T  **l**

Book 2: Axe Man

As always – to my wife, Polly and my son, Axel. You chase the shadows from my soul.

Once I said to a scarecrow, "You must be tired of standing in this lonely field."

And he said, "The joy of scaring is a deep and lasting one, and I never tire of it."

Said I, after a minute of thought, "It is true; for I too have known that joy."

Said he, "Only those who are stuffed with straw can know it."

Then I left him, not knowing whether he had complimented or belittled me.

Kahli Gibran

The Forever Man – Book 2
Prologue

The first pulse occurred in the old calendar year of 2022. A combination of planetary alignment, the Earth's rotation and the position of the sun combined to produce the perfect storm. A sequence of gigantic solar flares created a series of massive electromagnetic pulses that stopped the heart of our modern world.

America was struck first. And then, as the world turned, country by continent by hemisphere was returned to the dark ages. The wave of electromagnetic pulses destroyed all electrical and electronic equipment on the planet in an orgy of solar destruction. Airplanes fell to earth. Hospitals were plunged into darkness. Water supplies, controlled by electric valves and pumps ceased to flow. Backup generators burnt out. All communication. All transport. All machinery. Lights. Heating. It all died.

At the same time…so did our humanity.

And then they appeared . . .from the realms of fantasy, through a gateway formed by the pulse, came the trolls, the goblins and, leading them all – the Fair Folk. But were they here to help, or to conquer?

Chapter 1

Toilet paper. Twin ply. Super soft.

Nathaniel grinned to himself.

And coffee. Made with a machine. By a barista. Strong, bitter, honest to God coffee.

Thousands of years of human endeavor. Countless millions of man-hours of invention had been wiped out by the pulse. Computers. Space travel. Brain surgery. And what did The Forever Man miss the most? Something soft to wipe his ass with and a mildly addictive hot beverage made from the roasted seeds of the Rubiaceae bush.

Nathaniel's horse stumbled slightly. Weary from the days' riding. Snow crunched like broken glass beneath its hooves. The air resonant with the fragrance of pine resin and ozone overlaid by the subtle steel smell of newly minted snow. Gusts of wind shivered the trees, shaking clumps of white from their laden boughs. A giant baker dusting the land with icing sugar. Breath steamed from his open mouth in clouds of condensate, leeching the warmth from his core. Puff the magic dragon.

Winter had come across the land with a speed that baffled all. And it was the harshest winter in living memory. Nathaniel had heard theories that the unprecedented level of cold was brought about by the fact that there were no longer any factories left in the world. Nor heating of any sort. The cattle population had been decimated and there were no cars to fill the atmosphere with carbon monoxide. Global cooling had become a reality.

It had been over three months now since the first electromagnetic pulse had struck the earth. Destroying all electronic and electrical equipment in an orgy of solar destruction. And the pulses had continued on a daily basis, apparent by the almost constant glow of the Aurora Borealis, or Northern lights, in the sky, caused by the massive amounts of gamma radiation in the atmosphere.

But, apart from smashing mankind back into the dark ages, the gamma rays had also had another effect. Somehow they had changed marine master sergeant Nathaniel Hogan's DNA structure. They had enhanced his speed, strength and, most of all, his ability to heal. He was now capable of sustaining fatal wounds and recovering. However, he was still able to succumb to normal disease and starvation. He wasn't sure about drowning. Unfortunately he still felt pain. And normal common garden fatigue. But then one doesn't look an immortal horse in the mouth.

Nathaniel glanced down at the back of his left hand. The pink scar stood out like a brand.

He had dreamed of Stonehenge and druids one night and one of the druids had cut the symbol into his hand with a sickle. When he had awoken it was there. An ancient Traveling women had told him that it was the sign for Infinity and he had been marked as The Forever Man. And then she had shown him a small magik trick. Conjuring up fire with thought alone. She had told him to practice this every day as he had the gift. He had been doing so for almost two months now but to no avail. If the entire world hadn't become so topsy-turvy he would have dismissed her as a weirdo, but given the current circumstances he was loath to do so. She had also instructed him to go north to seek his destiny. This he was doing, and, in lieu of any other plan, he was happy to.

The marine decided to stop for the night and looked around for a likely spot, finally deciding on a fallen tree a little way off the beaten track. He hitched his horse to a tree, took out his collapsible shovel from one of the saddlebags and started to clear a spot, shoveling the snow aside and forming a low three foot wall in a horseshoe shape. When he had finished he spread a tarpaulin on the ground and then a couple of fur blankets. The blankets were black mink, as was the cloak that Nathaniel was wearing. He had come across a specialist fur shop in one of the small towns that he had traveled through and he had helped himself to half a dozen black minks. Then, with clumsy male stitching, he had converted two of the coats into a full-length cloak. The other four had become two separate blankets. It amused him that his little bivouac now contained over one hundred thousand dollars worth of fur at pre-pulse prices.

He spread another tarpaulin over the walls to make a low roof. Then he collected wood and kindling and built a small fire close to the entrance. The fire would keep the shelter warm and keep predators from coming inside. After that, before the light went, he placed five rabbit snares in likely looking places. Finally he took three skinned and dressed squirrels from his saddle bags, spitted them and placed them over the fire to cook whilst he took the saddle off the horse and rubbed it down before putting a blanket over him.

After he had eaten, Nathaniel fell into a deep and restful sleep. He awoke the next morning about half an hour before sunrise, stoked the fire and went to check the traps. Two had been successful and he took the rabbits back and skinned and gutted them. For breakfast he threw a couple of old potatoes into the fire and then he melted some snow in a pot for drinking water.

Finally he packed up, got back into the saddle and continued on his unplanned way.

As the day wore on he started to pass more and more houses. He stopped to check a few but they were mostly empty. And those that were not empty contained only corpses, desiccated and freeze dried from the sub zero temperatures. The lack of food, drugs and heating had taken a massive toll on the survivors of the initial pulse and now, a mere three months on, Nathaniel estimated that a full fifty percent of the population were dead. Over thirty million people.

Even so, he had expected to find some people in the houses. But the area was dead. Totally devoid of humanity.

Late that afternoon he came across the reason why. According to his map he was standing outside the rural village of Acton-on-vale. But what he saw in front of him looked nothing like a rural village. Running left to right the entire area was fenced in with steel reinforced concrete blast panels. Three meters high. Every one hundred yards a scaffold observation post rose another meter above the fence. Each observation post contained a soldier armed with a light machine gun. Far to his right he could see a steel gate. The gate was open and five armed guards stood in front of it. They were dressed in MTP camouflage and carried the SA80Mk3 assault rifles. One of them was already walking towards him, his weapon brought to bear.

Nathaniel dismounted and walked slowly towards the soldier, one hand on the horse's reins and the other held up above his head.

The approaching soldier seemed satisfied that he meant no harm and he lowered his rifle.

'Can I help?' He asked.

'Just passing through, lance corporal. Stopped to admire your wall.'

'You're welcome to come inside and take a look,' said the soldier. 'All are welcome as long as they obey then rules.' The soldier stared at Nathaniel for a moment and then asked. 'Is that a military uniform under your cloak?'

Nathaniel nodded. 'Master sergeant Nathaniel Hogan, United States Marine Corps.'

'The soldier came to attention, shouldering his rifle. 'Pleased to meet you, sir. I wonder if I might insist that you accompany me inside, sir. The Brigadier has ordered that all military personnel be introduced to him before they go on their way.'

'Lead the way, Lance corporal.'

Nathaniel led his horse and followed the lance corporal to the gate. When he got there two of the soldiers barred his way.

'Sorry, sir,' said the one. 'You need to check in all weapons before you go inside. We'll keep them safe and issue you with a ticket. Also, we'll take care of your horse. No horses allowed inside the perimeter.'

'Fair enough,' conceded Nathaniel. He pulled back his cloak and unholstered two sawn-off double-barrel shotguns that rode in hip holsters. Then he unsheathed a rifle from the horse's saddle. Finally he removed his double-headed battle-axe from the loop in his belt and handed it to one of the soldiers, then he hitched back his cloak so that it hung down his back, exposing his rank flashes. The soldier raised his one eyebrow but refrained from comment.

They wrote a receipt out in a small carbon book and gave Nathaniel a copy.

'With me, sir,' said the lance corporal.

The marine followed him as he walked through the open gates and headed towards the center of the village. He saw a few soldiers walking around and one or two civilians but on the whole, the place seemed remarkably empty.

'Where is everyone?' He asked.

'Working,' answered the lance corporal.

'Where?'

The soldier didn't answer and Nate couldn't be bothered to push him. He would ask the Brigadier.

Eventually they came to a massive Victorian rectory. Two armed men stood at attention outside the front door.

Nathaniel and the lance corporal mounted the stairs.

'Someone to see the brigadier,' said the lance.

The guards waved him through. The lance opened the front door and ushered Nate in, closing it behind him.

The entrance hall was huge, Persian carpets were scattered across the mahogany floor, large oils of landscapes and horses lined the walls. A fire crackled in the huge fireplace and the light from thirty or more candles reflected off the stupendous crystal chandelier.

The lance carried on through the hall and down a corridor, stopping at the second door and knocking twice.

Within seconds the door was opened by a tall, stooped, gray haired man sporting the uniform and flashes of a warrant officer class 1.

'Visitor for the brigadier, sir,' announced the lance.

The warrant officer nodded. 'Thank you, lance corporal. I'll take it from here.'

The lance swiveled on his heel and left.

The warrant officer waved Nathaniel into the room.

Nathaniel marched into the center of the room and came crashing to attention in front of the warrant officer and the brigadier. A short, wide man with cropped black hair and bristle moustache. He was dressed in combat uniform with his rank slide on his chest as opposed to shoulder badges. On his hip, a Glock 17.

The marine whipped up a solid parade ground salute, stood at rigid attention and bellowed in his best master sergeant voice.

'Marine corps master sergeant Nathaniel Hogan reporting as requested, sir.'

The brigadier's face registered his approval. 'At ease, mister Hogan.'

Nathaniel raised his right knee parallel to the floor and slammed it down as he shifted to the 'at ease' position, hands behind his back, thumbs interlocked, left in front of right.

'Stand easy, mister Hogan,' continued the brigadier.

Nathaniel relaxed almost imperceptibly apart from the fact that he now looked at the brigadier as opposed to straight ahead.

'So, soldier, what brings you here?' Asked the Brigadier.

'Simply passing through, sir.'

'We're looking for more soldiers, particularly non-comms. Could we interest you in staying?'

'With respect, sir,' answered Nathaniel. 'I would prefer to continue my journey.'

The Brigadier nodded. 'Fine, but I insist that you stay as our guest for two or three days. Take a look around, see what we're all about. Mayhap I can change your mind. Mister Clarkson here will show you to your quarters and issue you with the necessaries.'

The marine crashed to attention once more. 'Thank you, sir. Much appreciated.' He saluted again and followed warrant officer Clarkson out of the room.

Clarkson led him to the next room and ushered him in. He went over to a desk and pulled out a sheaf of papers, signed a few and handed them over.

'Here you go, mister Hogan These are permission slips. The yellow ones are for a day's accommodation, I have given you three. The green ones are for food. One meal per slip. I have allowed you two meals a day, breakfast and supper. Come with me and I'll show you to your digs.'

Nathaniel followed Clarkson out of the house, past the armed guards and down the road. Once again it struck the marine that there were next to no civilians present. He didn't bother to ask Clarkson where they were, figuring that he would find out later.

The snow had been cleared from all of the roads and pavements and there was no litter. Even the street signs had been cleaned and polished. All of these obvious pointers to the fact that the village was being militarily run.

After a few turns they came to a small Victorian terraced cottage. Clarkson opened the front door, which was unlocked and showed Nate in.

'Here you go, old chap. The water is running, we've set up a gravity feed tower, cold but drinkable and fine for washing in, if you're a complete Spartan. Please feel free to wander. If you'd like to go outside the perimeter one has to get permission from the Brigadier, I'm afraid. The officers' mess in the village hall, sure that you can find that by yourself. Any questions?'

Nathaniel shook his head. 'No, sir. All self-evident. Many thanks. Oh, maybe one, what about my horse?'

'Shouldn't worry about that, mister Hogan. The chaps will take good care of it.'

The warrant officer left, closing the door behind him as he did.

The marine took a walk through of the cottage. Two rooms downstairs, a sitting room and a kitchen. Off the kitchen was a small shower room and toilet. A stiff towel was hanging over the rail.

Narrow stairs to the first floor. At the top another two small rooms. Both rooms contained double beds. On the one bed was a set of linen. Sheets, a blanket, single thin pillow and a duvet. There were no personal items to be seen and Nathaniel wondered what had happened to the previous inhabitants.

He decided to take a shower, stripped down in the bedroom and laid his clothes out on the bed. His spare clothes were in his saddlebags on his horse so he would have to make do for the meanwhile.

Naked he walked down stairs, went into the bathroom and turned the shower on. The water was ice cold, only a little above freezing but he stepped in, grabbed the sliver of soap and, puffing and blowing, scrubbed himself down and rinsed off. He rubbed himself dry with the rough towel and jogged back up to the bedroom to get dressed, pulling his mink cloak tight around his shoulders until he had warmed up. Then he strapped on his boots and went outside.

He simply started to meander about the village without any special purpose. After a couple of turns he came across a large military tent pitched in a front garden. Steam billowed out of the side of the canvas structure and a strange smell of vinegar and sugar and fruit wafted through the air. He walked over to the open front of the tent to take a look. A single armed guard stood in the entrance. When he saw Nathaniel he nodded, obviously aware that he was around, but he said nothing.

The marine peered in to see a long row of villagers working over large catering pots that were suspended above cooking fires. Opposite them were another group of people working at a preparation table, slicing vegetables, peeling fruit, measuring and weighing. It didn't take him long to realize that they were pickling vegetables and turning fruit into preserves for the winter. Planning ahead. Everyone had their heads down, working hard, so he didn't talk to anyone. He simply watched for a short while and went on his way.

On the outskirts of the village in what looked like a horse paddock, he saw a large group of children, eight years to around twelve, marching around the arena. Instead of rifles they carried tools. Spades, garden forks, picks and shovels. A corporal called out time, berating those who fell out of step and complimenting those who marched straight and proud. The children wore khaki shirts and trousers and each had a square badge on their chest. A flag with a red cross of St. George and a sun and a moon in the top corners. On their right sleeves a small rectangular flash of white with the words, "The needs of the many outweigh the needs of the few".

The sight sent a shiver through the marine as memories of school history lessons and photo's of rows of Hitler Youth Children flashed through his mind.

The corporal saw the marine watching and beckoned to him to come over.

'Greetings, Master Sergeant,' he said. 'Taking a look at out budding troops, I see.'

Nathaniel nodded. 'Very impressive. Do they learn to shoot?'

'Oh yes. Field craft, weapon craft, doctrine, fitness, survival training. The Brigadier says that these are the future of our new world.'

'When do they get time for schooling?'

'They receive rudimentary reading, writing and arithmetic skills. The Brigadier believes that too much focus on intellectual pursuits will be damaging to their development as soldiers. Some of the more feeble ones, ones of less physical strength, are selected for more cerebral offerings.'

Nathaniel kept his face devoid of expression and simply nodded and went on his way.

Next he came across a group of four civilians, a man and three women of indeterminate middle age. Standing near them was an armed soldier. Two of the women were sweeping the snow off the roads and sidewalks and the other two were polishing the road signs. The soldier nodded a greeting but the civilians kept their eyes downcast and avoided looking at him as they concentrated on their menial tasks. As he drew away he heard one of them coughing, a deep wracking cough that sounded like the precursor of real problems.

Nathaniel continued his aimless stroll, noting that all of the signs were highly polished and the fences newly painted. The village was in parade ground condition. No longer a village and now an obvious military base. Once again he wondered where all of the inhabitants were.

He walked alongside the blast wall until he came to one of the sentry towers. It stood four meters high and was constructed from steel scaffolding. A ladder ran up the side to the platform.

Nathaniel gave the sentry a shout. 'Hey, soldier. Mind if I come up?'

The soldier peered over the side, took in the marine's rank and gave him a thumbs up. 'Help yourself, sir.'

He shimmied up the ladder and stepped onto the platform. The area was around six square yards, three-foot high railings and a 7.62 mm machine gun mounted on a swing mount that was attached to a steel stanchion.

The marine nodded to the soldier. 'Nathaniel Hogan, marine master sergeant.'

'Private Johnson, sir. Surrey territorials.'

Nathaniel pulled out a pack of cigarettes and offered. Johnson accepted with alacrity, a huge grin on his face.

'Thank you, sergeant. Ran out of these over a month ago. Commissioned officers only.'

Nathaniel lit for both of them and then gave the rest of the pack to the private.

'Here, take them. I've got more.'

Johnson slipped the pack into one of the pouches of his webbing, his face still agrin.

The two soldiers smoked in silence for a while and Nathaniel surveyed the land. About six hundred yards from the rear wall he could see a group of people working in a field, scraping the snow to one side and digging up something that looked like potatoes. Three armed guards stood close by them. He also noticed small groups walking through the forest. Groups of threes and fours. Each with a soldier.

'What are they doing?' He asked Johnson.

'Laying traps, sir. Rabbits, birds, small game. The meat is brought back and either used straightaway or smoked and salted for storage. Also general forage, wild carrots, tubers, fruits. The Brigadier has set up a system. We need to be fully self sustaining ASAP. No relying on old generation tinned foods and such, sir. We are the new generation.'

Nathaniel dragged on his cigarette. Said nothing.

'These people owe a lot to the Brigadier,' continued Johnson. 'We were on exercises in the area, using the local base, only a couple of hundred of us. The bulk of the boys were in Afghanistan when the power went. Within a day the Brigadier had a plan, reckoned that the base was indefensible as well as being unsustainable. So we decamped to this village. If it weren't for us it they would all have starved. Now we have food being stored for the winter, running water, defenses. The continuation of our civilization. And it won't stop here. In time we can expand, bring more people under rule. Make more people safe.'

Nathaniel nodded. Whatever he thought, it was obvious that the Brigadier had achieved a great deal in a small amount of time.

'Right then,' he said to Johnson. 'Thanks for the info. See you later.'

He climbed back down the tower and continued his circuit of the wall finally ending up at the village green.

There was a large army tent erected in the middle of the green and he could see through the entrance that it was full of trestle tables and a variety of chairs. Most of the tables were full of people sitting down and eating and there were still long queues at the chow line as people waited patiently, bowls in hand, to get some sustenance.

Nathaniel could smell the food from where he stood and it seemed to consist mainly of boiled turnips, potato and cabbage. Way in the background a slight smell of meat. Probably rabbit. The villagers looked lethargic, faces pale and movements slow. Whenever he caught someone's eye they immediately looked down, their faces showing obvious fear.

The marine contemplated missing dinner as the smell of boiling turnips was turning his stomach, but he hadn't eaten since that morning so he figured that he had better try to get something into his belly while he had the chance.

He continued past the green to the village hall where Clarkson had told him the officers' mess was. The front doors were closed and he let himself in. The first thing that struck him was the atmosphere. Someone, a young girl it seemed, was playing a piano in the corner. Classical renditions of pop songs. The place was well lit with candles and mirrors and a fire crackled away in the hearth, filling the place with warmth. And the smell of the food immediately made his mouth water.

Fried chicken, mashed potato with butter, peas, gravy, corn. There were bottles of red wine at the tables as well as jugs of water and fresh fruit juice. It was as if he had entered another world. A world of privilege and power. And then he realized; that is exactly what he had done. Outside were the new world peasants. The grubbers of dirt and the wielders of plows. And in this room were the leaders of the elite. Soldiers. Warriors. Men with power.

Nathaniel took a deep breath and walked into the room.

The brigadier, who was sitting at the top table, saw him and beckoned to him.

'Mister Hogan. Join us.'

The marine walked over and sat down next to the commanding officer.

'So, mister Hogan,' continued the Brigadier. 'You've had a good look around. What do you think.'

'I'm a sergeant, sir,' responded the marine. 'Not my job to think.'

The Brigadier smiled. But only with his lips, no humor touched his eyes. 'I give you permission to think. Go ahead.'

'Very efficiently run outfit, sir,' said Nathaniel. 'Not sure if I'd want to be a civilian.'

The brigadier raised an eyebrow. 'Why?'

'Well, sir, never been one for grubbing in the dirt and surviving on turnip soup.'

The brigadier nodded. 'I see. You appear to have come across the lower echelons being fed. The tent on the green. Yes,' agreed the brigadier. 'It's a tough life for them. However, better than being dead one might say. But what you do not know, mister Hogan, is those were only a part of the community. The lowest and least skilled of the village. There is another kitchen closer to the gates where the middle echelons are fed. Those are the people with more discernable skills. Blacksmiths, engineers, farmers, farriers and such. Their fare is substantially better than turnip soup.'

'As good as this?'

The brigadier laughed. 'Of course not. We are officers. The enlisted men get similar food, no booze. But the middle echelons get a meat ration and bread with their soup. An adequate amount of calories to survive and to work.'

'There seem to be many empty houses, sir. Casualties?'

'No,' answered the brigadier. 'Thanks to us there were very few casualties in the village. We've had, perhaps, a ten percent die back. Diabetics, people whom were on various life giving drugs that ran out, the elderly. The empty houses are part of the new order. One is assigned housing depending on one's usefulness to the community as a whole. The lower echelons share housing. Four to a room, male and females separated. The middles echelons get their own house, ranging from a three bedroom for the farrier down to smaller one or two beds for farmers and assistants. The doctor has a very decent digs as does the priest.'

'As do you, sir,' interjected Nathaniel.

'Yes, I am the commanding officer. My place used to belong to a city trader. Now he is one of the lower echelons. Good for nothing but wielding a spade. No discernable skills whatsoever.'

'And what are the empty houses for then?' Enquired the marine.

'Newcomers, such as yourself,' said the brigadier. 'We accept all comers, interview them, allocate them a job and in return they get food, shelter and safety.'

Someone put a full plate of food down in front of the marine and he concentrated on getting it inside him. The brigadier sat silently for a while, sipping on a glass of red wine. After a minute or so he stood up. Immediately everyone in the room stood to attention.

The brigadier waved them back down. 'As you were, gentlemen. I grow weary and shall take my leave.' He left the hall followed closely by his two armed guards and everyone sat down and continued with their meals.

Warrant officer Clarkson, who was sitting on Nathaniel's left side, offered the marine a glass of wine. He nodded his thanks.

'He's a great man, you know,' said Clarkson. 'What you see is just the beginning. Soon we shall start to expand our net. Bring in more villages and towns under us, set up communications via fast horse. Expand the central army to include a militia. Create centralized farms and production units. Everyone will have equal access to food and shelter.'

'Except for the military,' rejoined Nathaniel.

'Well, obviously, yes. For any civilization to achieve, one must have a ruling class.'

The marine said nothing.

'You seem skeptical, master sergeant.'

'I don't know if skeptical is the correct word,' answered Nathaniel. 'Perhaps incredulous is closer.'

'Why?'

'Military rule? Armies are run to fight wars, not to rule civilizations. Look at Hitler, Adi Amin, Stalin, Genghis Kahn. Power can be gained by the barrel of a gun but never held by it.'

'You misunderstand, master sergeant. We do not seek to conquer. We seek to help. We have no political agenda at all.'

'War is the continuation of politics,' argued Nathaniel. 'And before you say that you aren't at war let me tell you – you are. What would happen if you stood your soldiers down and disarmed them?'

'Obviously there might be a breakdown of discipline,' admitted Clarkson.

Nathaniel snorted. 'A breakdown of discipline? The people would rise up and bloody slaughter the lot of you.'

Clarkson shook his head vehemently. 'No way, master sergeant. They understand that what we are doing is for the best. The needs of the many outweigh the needs of the few. As I say, a few may become a little undisciplined but not much more.'

'Bullshine,' said Nathaniel. 'They won't even look a soldier in the eye. They're all living in terror. You have taken their houses and split up their families and dine on fried chicken whilst they subsist on turnip water. Wake up, man.'

Clarkson had gone pale with rage as he stared at Nathaniel. 'Master sergeant,' he said. 'You are dismissed. You are no longer welcome in the officers' mess. Please leave this instant.'

Nathaniel stood up. 'I'm sorry, mister Clarkson. I didn't mean to offend. Especially after being given such a welcome. It was churlish of me in the extreme. I shall leave first thing in the morning after extending my thanks to the Brigadier.'

He bowed and walked slowly from the hall and into the night. A light snow was falling; little eddies of wind causing it to swirl about the marine's head like moths around a flame.

He took out a cigarette, cupped his hands against the wind and lit up. Then he walked back to his digs, deep in thought. He didn't know why he was so riled up. Most of what Clarkson said was true; the bulk of the villagers would have died by now if left to their own devices. The brigadier had created a safe haven in a world gone mental. The bulk of the villagers were eating, albeit subsistence rations. But the whole thing stank like a nine-day-old kipper. Sometimes, just because you could do something, was no real reason to go ahead and do it. One thing was for sure; the brigadier was on one huge power trip. Nevertheless, thought Nathaniel, whilst the situation was not to his liking it wasn't actually broken. People were safe and alive, far be it for him to blunder in righting wrongs that were not even considered wrongs by many of the people involved.

He arrived at his digs and stood outside for a while, dragging on the remains of his cigarette. As he finished, the door of a cottage three down from his crashed open and two soldiers stepped out. Between them was a young girl. Perhaps fifteen or maybe sixteen. It was hard to tell in the dark but it looked as if she had been weeping. Behind her was an older man, gray hair, spectacles.

'You can't do this,' the older man said. His voice a desperate plea.

'Brigadier's orders,' replied the one soldier. 'Now stand back.'

The older man lunged forward and grabbed the girl, attempting to pull her from the soldier's grasp. The soldier who had spoken before, casually smashed his elbow into the man's face, splitting the flesh below his eye and knocking him to the ground, sending his spectacles flying.

Nathaniel strode over. 'What's going on here?' He asked.

'Back off, 'retorted the soldier.

'Back off – sergeant,' bellowed the marine.

The soldier came to attention. 'Sorry, sergeant,' he said. 'My mistake. Thought that you were a civvie. Brigadier's orders, sergeant. He said to bring the girl to his quarters.'

'Why?'

The private shrugged. 'Not mine to ask, sergeant. Not in this man's army. Brigadier commands and I do.'

Nathaniel nodded. It was the answer that he expected. A private was a mere pawn in an institution where crap ran downhill so he was constantly covered in the stuff. Every crappy job went to the lowest ranks first.

'As you were, private,' he said. 'Just make sure that no harm comes to the girl.'

Once again the private shrugged. 'It will or it won't, sergeant, but I can assure you, I will not harm her.'

The two soldiers dragged the weeping girl off.

Nathaniel picked up the older man's spectacles and handed them to him.

The man accepted them with shaking hand. 'How could you?' He said. 'She's but a child. She's my granddaughter. Barely fifteen years old.'

'I'm sure that she'll be fine,' replied Nathaniel.

The old man shook his head. 'I know that you've just got here, but how can you be so naïve? What do you think is happening here? Do you think that monster has invited her over for milk and cookies?'

Nathaniel turned and started to walk back to his digs.

The old man grabbed his cloak. 'He's going to rape her. He's going to take my little girl and tear her clothes off and beat her and rape her.' He started to weep. Quietly. Then he let go of the marine's cloak and simply sat down in the snow, tears running down his cheeks. 'He's going to rape her and there's nothing that I can do.'

The marine stood and watched him for a while. Thoughts tumbled through his mind. The needs of the many outweigh the needs of the few. These people had shelter. Food. Protection from the roving gangs. But who would protect them from their protectors? And why should it be his problem? He would go back to his house, sleep, get up tomorrow and go. Leave well enough alone.

The old man held his head in his hands and rocked back and forth slightly. A picture of utter dejection.

'Oh damn it,' said Nate,' as he turned and started to stride towards the brigadier's house. 'I know that I'm going to regret this.'

It took him less than two minutes to reach the brigadier's house and he walked straight up to the front door. The two ever-present guards blocked his way.

'Sorry, sergeant,' said the one. 'No entrance. The brigadier is busy for the evening.'

'No,' said Nate. 'Not anymore.' He grabbed the guard's rifle and pulled the man towards him, arched his back and delivering a crashing head butt to the bridge of the man's nose. He dropped to the floor like a sack of wheat. Nate ripped the rifle from his inert fingers, swung on his heel and smacked the butt into the other guard's temple, dropping him in the same manner.

Then he opened the door and walked in. He figured that the brigadier would be upstairs and he ran up the sweeping marble staircase to the next floor. He entered a corridor with a row of doors along one side and a set of double doors at the very end. Nate reckoned that the double doors were probably the entrance to the master suit so he went straight to them and kicked them open.

The girl was naked and tied to the bed. The brigadier, still in full dress uniform, stood over her with a riding crop. The red swollen weals that criss-crossed the girl's torso spoke of mute testament as to what the brigadier was doing.

He turned to face Nate, his face a picture of absolute surprise.

'What the bloody hell?' He exclaimed. 'How dare you, sergeant? Get out.'

Nate raised the rifle and pointed it at the brigadier. 'You filthy old animal, put the whip down and untie the girl.'

The brigadier's face went purple with rage. 'Put the rifle down this instant. You are addressing a superior officer.'

'No I'm not,' said Nate. 'I'm merely addressing an officer that outranks me. Now do as I say or I swear that I'll shoot your dick off.'

But the brigadier could still not get past the enormity of being addressed in such a way by a mere non-commissioned officer, so he simply shook his head and shouted, 'guards!'

Nate, who was not one to issue idle threats, flicked the safety off the rifle and fired a round into the floor next to the officer's feet. 'Untie her, or the next one will leave you singing soprano for the rest of your life.'

The officer stepped over to the bed and quickly untied the girl.

'Where are her clothes?' Asked Nate.

The brigadier pointed to a pile in the corner.

'Get dressed, sweetheart,' said Nate. 'What's your name?'

'Stacey,' she replied. Her voice shaking.

Okay, Stacey, quickly now, get dressed and then come and stand by me.'

The girl did as she was told and then stood behind Nate.

'What now?' She asked.

'Damned if I know, Stacey.' answered Nate. 'I'm making this up as I go along.' He used his rifle to motion towards the door. 'Come on, brigadier. Outside, you first.'

The brigadier opened the door and walked out. Nate followed and, as he stepped out into the corridor, a sixth sense told him to move. He stared to pull back but it was too late. A rifle butt smashed into his cheek, splitting the skin and knocking him down. Immediately a veritable herd of boots started kicking him. At least five men, crowding in close and giving it all that they had. He felt his nose break with a gravel-like crunch. Then he distinctly heard at least three ribs and a collarbone break. Dry dull snapping sounds.

As he passed out he found just enough time to berate himself for being such an idiot.

***

The sun rose over a crisp, white land. The sky was a clear frigid blue and a light wind stirred little flurries of snow from the ground like a restless child at play.

A man pushed through the crowd. He was holding a bucket of water that he chucked over another man who was tied with his back to a wooden stake in the middle of the village green.

Nate choked and spluttered as the icy water yanked him from unconsciousness. Pain washed over him in waves as he pulled against his restraints. He looked around to see that the whole village was there plus all of the soldiers. In front of them all stood mister Clarkson and the brigadier.

'Last night,' said the brigadier. 'This man was apprehended by my loyal soldiers while he was attempting to rape a young girl from our village.'

There were a couple of muted denials from the crowd that were swiftly quashed by some aggressive stares from both the brigadier and mister Clarkson.

'We offered this man our home and in return he decided to violate our children, our most precious recourse. As you all know, I am a fair ruler. Sometimes hard, but always fair. And I have made it obvious that, in this brave new world of ours, there are certain crimes that carry with them the very harshest penalties. Murder, rape and theft are capital crimes and, as such, their wages are death. This is for the good of all. We cannot allow our society to slip into anarchy. The good of the many outweighs the good of the few. I therefore decree that this man, Nathaniel Hogan, be put to death by gunshot. As is the custom the penalty shall be carried out by myself as I have no wish to put the death of others onto the conscience of my people.'

The brigadier stood before Nate and drew his Browning pistol.

'Do you have any last words, mister Hogan?'

Nathaniel smiled as he looked at the brigadier. 'Yep, enjoy your last few hours on this planet. Because, before midday tomorrow, I'm going to have your head on a stick, you megalomaniacal asshole.'

'Don't be ridiculous,' retorted the brigadier. 'I don't accept threats from a dead man.'

Nate winked. 'Tomorrow, midday. It's a date.'

The brig pointed his weapon at Nate's chest and pulled the trigger twice. The high velocity nine-millimeter rounds slammed Nate back against the wooden stake, smashing and tearing through his lungs as his dead body slumped down against the restraints and hung there. A sacrifice. A warning.

'Leave him there,' said the brigadier. 'Let them all see what happens to those who transgress my laws.'

It started to snow. The flakes whispered down from the leaden sky and covered the dead marine in a shroud of ice.

And in the background Stacey wept softly as her grandfather comforted her.

Chapter 2

The Fair-Folk together with their Orcs, goblins, trolls and constructs had occupied a combined area of round four square miles. The entire area had been fenced in with a wooden stockade and a nearby stream and been diverted through the massive encampment to provide water.

The council of mages, whom were now operating at full power due to the massive concentrations of life-light on the new planet, had set up an area of Glamour. The glamouring spell discouraged people from noticing the encampment. It didn't make it invisible; it simply suggested that you ignore it. And up to now the spell had worked remarkably well.

Two cycles of the moon had passed since commander Ammon Set-Bat had led his people from their dying planet. Their planet had once had been continually bathed in solar flares and gamma ray energy but, due to a solar shift, the pulses had stopped and so had the gamma rays. And gamma radiation, or what the Fair-Folk referred to as the 'Life-Light' was what they used to power their magiks. And without their magik the Fair-Folk were a diminished people. But chief mage, Seth Hil-Nu, had ventured far and wide, through both time and space and dimensions seeking another compatible place and time. And he had discovered earth. They had created a gateway and the entire civilization had been transferred. Fair-Folk, battle Orcs, Goblins, Trolls and the Constructs.

As well as the glamoring the circle of mages had charged all with a universal spell of communication. It allowed all of the members of their peoples to understand and communicate with the Earth people.

This also seemed to be working well, although they had not used it much, the biggest problem being that the spell enhanced communicative abilities but it could do little about inherent intelligence. Therefore, the Orcs could communicate but only in a very rudimentary way. The goblins were their usual quick, duplicitous selves and the trolls were as simple and uncommunicative as before.

Commander Ammon had sent out small detachments of Orcs and goblins to scout the far outlying areas and they were returning with mixed reports. There were a few constants; during all sightings and meetings between the two species the earth people reacted with fear and shock. And sometimes with aggression.

They had been there for almost two months now and Ammon had decided that the time had come to plan an expansion. After all, they were not in this new world simply to survive, they were here to thrive. So the commander had stepped up the amount and the range of the scouting parties that he sent out. Sometimes there were upward of over twenty fast battle squads of groups. Each group consisted of five battle Orcs and five goblin archers. One of the Orcs would have the rank of dekado, leader of ten, and one of the goblins would be a quinto, second in charge. Their primary role was one of reconnaissance and fact finding and they were encouraged to avoid hostilities if possible.

***

Orc sergeant Nog sniffed at the air, his nose flaps pulsing in and out. The smell of human was strong. Many human. Close by. The Orc turned to his goblin corporal.

'Human,' he grunted. 'Many human. Near to us.'

Corporal Rames nodded. His sense of smell was not as acute as the Orc and he accepted his findings without question.

The battle squad moved forward, cautiously coming out of the cover of the forest. In front of them were a group of seven or so humans, a mixture of male and female. It looked as though they were tilling the fields. Working with hoe and shovel. Nog and his group had come across groups of humans before and every one had taken one look at them and ran away in terror.

But these humans were different.

One of the males looked up and saw the battle group walking towards them. He stopped hoeing and stared for a few seconds before speaking to his fellow farmers. They all stopped what they were doing and watched the battle group approach.

The male that had first noticed the group walked towards Nog.

'Greetings, travelers,' he said. 'I have heard rumors but this is the first time that I have actually seen any of you. My name is Basil, although I prefer to be known as Sunbeam.'

The Orc tilted his head to one side. 'I am Nog. I prefer to be known as Nog because that is who I am.'

'Cool, Nog,' said Basil as he held his hand out to shake.

Nog stared at the human's outstretched hand and decided to ignore it, not sure what he was doing.

'We are scouting the land,' rumbled the Orc. 'We are not looking for conflict and mean no harm.'

'That's cool, dude,' responded Basil. 'We are a commune of like-minded individuals. Vegans of course.

Would you and your companions like to eat with us? I would very much like to talk.'

Nog nodded and beckoned to his squad who formed up behind him.

Lunch consisted of a large vegetable curry. Nog pushed at his with his thick claws. 'No meat.' He said.

'We are vegans,' explained Basil. 'We eat no meat nor use animal product or the labors of animals.'

The Orc pushed his bowl away. 'Then soon you will all die. No fur coats, no shoes, no honey to make mead. You will all be dead by the fifth winter.'

Basil shook his head. 'No, we will persevere. And we shall do so without exploiting animals.'

Nog stood up. 'No, you will all die. You are all very stupid. Thank you for the meal. It contained little nourishment but your offer showed kindness.'

The squad left with Nog.

'These thin-skins are strange in the extreme,' he said to Rames. 'Truly they must be simple to think that they are the same as animals.

'Their females are very attractive, though,' said the goblin.

'Yes,' agreed Nog. 'Even more than the finest constructs.'

Taking Nog's lead the squad started jogging, heading back to their new home to report.

***

Corporal Owen Soames took another bite of rabbit. Chewed. Swallowed.

'Sick of rabbit,' he said.

'Tough,' said corporal Robbie Robson. 'Cause there's lots of them and they're easy to catch.'

'Heard that you can starve to death on rabbit. No matter how much you eat.'

'Naw,' disagreed Robbie. 'That's bullshit and you know it. As long as we eat other stuff with it we'll be fine. It's just that the body can't process too much lean meat.'

Whatever,' said Owen. 'Bored with rabbit. Want a Big Mac. Fries. Strawberry milkshake.'

Robbie laughed. 'Me too.'

The two corporals were from 21 SAS and had been involved in an evade and capture exercise in Cornwall when the pulse struck. It hadn't taken them long to figure out what had happened and their next decision had been relatively simple. Neither had any family and there was no way that they were going to hump all the way to Herefordshire HQ merely to find the place deserted. So, they decided to take a well-earned break and simply set up camp where they were.

Water and small game were plentiful and, after a few foraging exercises into abandoned houses, they now had a good supply of alcohol and cigarettes. To men used to absolute extremes of discomfort they were now living in comparative luxury and had been doing so for almost three months now. They had eschewed the idea of taking over an actual house or barn as, firstly, they preferred sleeping outdoors and, secondly, it made tactical sense in a possible hostile environment to keep low and keep moving.

Owen finished off his rabbit, threw the bones into the fire and drew a pack of cigarettes from his webbing. He was about to light up when Robbie raised a hand. Owen reacted instantly, slipping the cigs back into their pouch, kicking snow over the fire and bringing his weapon, an HK53 short assault rifle, to his shoulder.

Robbie slid over to him and whispered. 'Something out there,' he pointed to the forest. 'Lots of somethings, actually. Grab your kit and let's move.'

Within seconds the two SAS soldiers had packed up and were moving stealthily through the trees and the snow. They broke out of the tree line and, keeping low, headed for a small rocky torr that stuck up out of the snow about a hundred yards away, climbing it and nestling in amongst the boulders, unseen.

Robbie, who was carrying an L11A2 sniper rifle fitted with a set of Schmidt & Bender telescopic sights, used the sights to scope out the tree line. Owen did the same thing using his set of Mil-Tech binoculars.

Robbie spotted them first.

'Good God.'

'What?' Asked Owen.

'There, on your left, behind the big Oak tree.'

Owen swiveled and focused. 'What the hell are those?'

'Don't know,' replied Robbie. 'Looks like they're wearing some sort of gray body armor. Full-face helmet. Carrying swords and shields.'

'Oh come on, no ways,' exclaimed Owen. 'Look behind them. The dudes carrying bows and arrows.'

Robbie adjusted his sight line. 'What the hell…'

'I'll tell you what the hell,' said Owen. 'They are goblins. And trolls, or maybe Orcs.'

'Like Lord of the Rings?' Asked Robbie.

'Exactomundo, Robbie. Middle earth, hobbits, elves, the whole bleeding thing.'

'That's impossible,' said Robbie.

'Apparently not,' countered Owen. 'Because there they are.'

'So what now?'

'Well,' considered Owen. 'If they really are Orcs and goblins then, according to popular belief, they would be the baddies.'

'And we would be the goodies?' Questioned Robbie.

'That would be correctomundo, Robbie.'

'So what do we do?'

'I reckon that we lie here and do nothing. Who knows what that bunch are capable of. Tough looking buggers if I ever saw any.'

The two SAS men lay still for a while. Observing.

Suddenly Robbie spoke. 'Aw, crap. They've seen us.'

'How?'

'I don't know. But they have. Look, here they come.'

The battle squad started running towards the two soldiers. Churning through the snow, swords held aloft as they came.

'I'll try a warning shot,' said Robbie as he chambered a round into the breech of his sniper rifle. He aimed and fired, kicking up a fountain of snow in front of the lead Orc.

The squad kept coming, except for the goblins who all immediately stopped running, fitted arrows to their bows and fired. The shafts clattered off the rocks around the SAS men.

'Sod that,' said Robbie. 'No one shoots arrows at this soldier.' He drew a bead on the foremost Orc and pulled the trigger. The high velocity, full metal jacket round struck the Orc in the center of his chest. He took two more steps and then fell to the ground. Robbie swiveled and fired again, dispatching the next Orc.

Next to him, Owen opened up with his HK53. Short bursts, moving right to left, knocking the Orcs down.

Another hail of arrows fell around the two of them and Robbie turned his attention to the goblins, cycling and firing at a steady pace. By the time that he had fired eight times the battle group were all dead. Lying still on the white snow. He noted that their blood was as red as his own. For some reason that made him feel uncomfortable.

Robbie stood up. 'Come on,' he said. 'Let's check this out.' He started walking towards the fallen and Owen followed close behind.

Owen knelt down next to one of the Orcs and prodded its arm. 'Man, these guys are built.' He pulled back the Orc's tunic to expose the gunshot wound that had killed it. 'And take a look at this. Its skin must be at least two inches thick. Hell, I'd hate to sit on this guys bar stool by mistake.' He stood up. 'This is insane. I mean, where did they come from?' He turned to face Robbie. 'What do you...'

Owen never finished his sentence as a yard long arrow thudded into his chest, the barbed point penetrating his entire body and sticking out of his back. He looked down at it in disbelief.

'Oh, crapola. No way. Killed by a bloody arrow. That sucks.' He fell to his knees and pitched sideways. Dead before he hit the snow.

Robbie looked up to see another battle group charging at him, coming from the woods. He raised his rifle, sighted. Fired. Once, got one. Twice, missed. Empty. He had committed the cardinal sin of not reloading after the first skirmish.

He grinned to himself. Just as well sergeant MacFadden wasn't here, he thought. He'd kill me for making such a rookie mistake. Mind you, he continued his thought. Looks like he'd have to queue up to get to me.

He dropped the rifle and drew his Glock 17, racked the slide, aimed at the foremost Orc and fired. The nine-millimeter round barely slowed the creature down. Robbie fired again, six times in quick succession and the Orc dropped. He swiveled and fired at the next one, banging away until it dropped. He was out of ammo again so he dropped the pistol and pulled out his assault knife.

An Orc moved in close, swinging its massive sword at Robbie's head. The soldier ducked and rammed his blade into the Orcs torso, under his arm, twisting hard as he did so. The Orc squealed and pulled away but Robbie couldn't wrench his knife free. Another Orc jumped forward and struck Robbie on the head with its shield. Then it followed up with a massive overhead swipe of its sword. The huge blade almost cut Robbie in half, killing him instantly.

The Orc that he had stabbed grunted a few times and then slowly keeled over. Dead.

The remaining Orc and the five goblins checked the soldier's bodies to ensure that they were dead. None of them attempted to pick up their weapons or check the bodies for valuables. To do so was taboo and would result in bad favor in the next battle.

'Those thin skins were tough fighters,' said the Orc.

One of the goblins shrugged. 'Their far weapons are great. But when you get close they are no match.'

The Orc tilted his head to one side. 'That one killed Pok using only his little knife. That not easy. If he had sword or axe might have been different. Might have killed us all. They very agile. Fast. Also kill without compunction. Dangerous. We must report back.'

The goblin agreed. 'Yes, we must. Let's go,'

The remnants of the second battle group formed up and started to run.

Chapter 3

Stacey knelt down and placed the twig of witch hazel in front of the snow-covered marine's body. It's small red blooms looked like blood against the white of the snow. The young teenager checked around to make sure that no soldiers had seen her and started to stand up.

'Hey, Stacey,' whispered Nate.

She squealed and fell over backwards.

'Quiet, darling,' continued Nathaniel. 'We don't want to draw any attention, do we?'

'But you're dead,' said Stacey.

'Apparently not,' replied the marine.

'But I saw you get shot. We all did. Everybody saw you die.'

'Oh well, looks can be deceiving. Look, do you want to untie me here? I've got a hot date with a brigadier and I'd hate to be late.'

Stacey crawled behind Nate and pulled at his bonds, working hard at the frozen rope. Eventually she worked the knots loose, Nate pulled his arms free and stood up.

'Thanks Stacey,' he said as he gave her a quick hug. 'Now go home. Things are going to be happening here. Not sure how safe it will be for a while.'

The young girl nodded and ran off. Nate headed for the guardhouse. He wanted his weapons back, particularly the axe.

A light snow started to fall as he made his way along the fence towards the front gate, deadening sound and kicking up the chill factor. When he got to the front guardhouse he eschewed any form of subtlety and simply walked straight up to the first guard, Then, before the guard could even issue a challenge, Nate jerked his rifle from his hands and smashed the butt into his temple dropping him like an ugly stepchild. Then the marine stepped into the guardhouse and dispatched the remaining two guards in similar fashion. Clinically and efficiently.

He couldn't remember the ticket number that his weapons were stored under but there were only ten lockers and they were unlocked, so he simply took a quick look through them. His axe and shotguns were in the fifth locker, so he removed them, strapped them on and strode from the room, heading for the brigadiers residence.

The marine didn't have much of a plan, but he did have one. It was fairly simple; kill the brigadier, then appoint a new commanding officer who would rule in conjunction with some sort of civilian committee.

When he reached the residence the two guards at the door barred his way neither of them putting together the fact that this was the same man who was meant to be dead and tied to a stake on the village green.

Nate pulled out his axe and laid left and right, twisting the blade at the last moment so that the flat side hit the guards in the head, dropping them to the ground. He kicked open the front door and strode in, heading towards the brigadiers office at the end of the corridor.

The door was open sop the marine walked in. The brigadier was sitting behind his desk and warrant officer Clarkson stood opposite.

When they realized who had just walked into the room the looks of utter astonishment on their faces was almost comic.

Mister Clarkson simply stared at Nate, pointed and made an incomprehensible sound at the back of his throat. A combination between a gargle and a low cry of terror.

But the brigadier, who was made of sterner stuff, stood up and berated the marine.

'How dare you walk in here unannounced? You're meant to be dead. Leave my office at once. Guards!'

'The guards are indisposed,' said Nate. 'And now, as promised, it's time to put your head on a stick.'

The brigadier went for his pistol. But he was slow. Very slow. As slow as death.

Nathaniel's axe whipped through the air and struck the brigadier at the juncture where his neck met his chest. The officer's head seemed to leap from his shoulders and a jet of deep crimson blood arced out and sprayed the walls and the floor with gay abandon.

Nathaniel turned to mister Clarkson who had both his hands held up above his head.

'No,' he said. 'He made me do it. I wanted him to stop, it wasn't my fault.'

'Yes it was,' said Nate. 'You aided him. You abetted him. And now you shall join him,'

The axe sang it's song again, cleaving through Clarkson's upraised arms and his neck. Bathing the room in blood and body parts.

Nate wiped his axe on the curtains and then picked up the two heads, holding them by their hair, then he headed for the village green where he had been shot and left for dead. He knew that now was the most dangerous time. He had to keep a certain momentum going or else the soldiers would simply shoot him and then decide for themselves what to do next.

He made the green in under a minute. The first thing that he did was cast Clarkson's head on the ground in front of the stake that they had tied the marine to. Secondly, he jammed the brigadier's head onto the top of the stake. Brigadier on a stick.

Thirdly he drew one of his shotguns and fired twice into the air.

Then he pegged the tips of the axe into the turf, lent against the shaft, and waited.

Soldiers arrived first, both privates and officers. Then villagers, in singles and groups.

Nathaniel stood straight and proud, his look commanding. Unflinching. For he knew that his demeanour was all that would keep the situation under control. A man with grey hair and a clipped moustache, sporting a major's crown on his chest, marched up to Nate. Close behind him was another younger man with the three captains pips.

The major spoke first. 'What the hell is going on here? How come you're still alive? Who did that to the brigadier and mister Clarkson?'

Nathaniel stood to attention and cracked out a perfect salute.

'Master sergeant Nathaniel Hogan, sir. Definitely not dead, sir. On account of being immortal, sir.'

'Don't be silly, sergeant. Nobody is immortal.'

'Appears that I am, sir,' continued Nate in his best high volume parade ground voice. 'Something to do with the electrical pulse, sir. Long story, perhaps we can discuss it later, sir?'

The major nodded, his expression more than a little puzzled. 'Carry on.'

'Sir,' continued the marine. 'Last night I witnessed the brigadier attempting to rape and beat an under aged female villager. When I attempted to stop the brigadier I was set upon, tied up and shot, as you know. This morning, when I had healed up, I went to the brigadier and mister Clarkson and voiced my displeasure to them. The brigadier went for his weapon and I was forced to defend myself. The result of which you see on this stick here, sir.'

The major stared at Nate for a while. 'The brigadier said that he had caught you attempting to rape the young lady,' he said.

'Foul lies, sir,' retaliated Nate. He pointed out Stacey in the crowd. 'Ask the lady in person, sir. She'll tell you.'

The major turned to face the young girl who nodded. 'It was the brigadier,' she said, her voice clear and loud.

There was a swell of noise from the villagers who started to surge forward. The soldiers immediately brought their weapons to bear, their faces taut with nervousness.

'Stand down, men,' shouted the major. 'What do you have in mind, sergeant?'

'A committee, sir,' replied Nate. 'Six strong consisting of three villagers and three military. The military being one officer, yourself, a non-commissioned officer and an enlisted man. The civilians to have at least one woman. Food and rations to be equally shared amongst all and housing facilities to be reissued in a fairer way.'

'Or else what?'

'There is no, or else, sir. It simply makes sense, both morally and tactically. Hearts and minds, sir.'

The major nodded. 'I agree.' He turned to face the villagers. 'People, as you probably all know, I am major Robert Soames. You have all heard what the marine has advised and I, for one, agree. I put it to you that you all get together and elect yourselves a trio of representatives. I then propose that we meet in the main house in an hour and take it from there.'

There was a general murmur of agreement from the crowd.

The major nodded at Nathaniel. 'Well, sergeant,' he said. 'You appear to have brought the winds of change with you. Will you join us at the house?'

Nate shook his head. 'No, sir. If you don't mind I think that I will sit this one out. I won't be staying and shouldn't have anything to do with who is elected. Not my place.'

'You seemed to think that it was your place to decapitate the brigadier.'

'That was different, sir,' responded Nate. 'After all, he did shoot me.'

'True,' admitted the major. 'But don't leave without seeing me.'

'Will do, sir,' replied Nate as he threw out another salute.

The major turned and walked away, followed by the rest of the soldiers. The villagers crowded around Nathaniel, patting him on the back and shaking his hand. Stacey ran up to him and threw her arms around him.

'Thank you, Nate,' she said, kissing him on both cheeks.

After a while the marine extricated himself. 'Listen, guys,' he said. 'I'm going back to my digs. I'm going to have a shower and take a rest. I'll see you all later.'

He walked off to more backslapping and high fives as he went.

Chapter 4

Commander Ammon Set-Bat and chief mage Seth Hil-Nu sat in a large two-seater palanquin that was carried by eight orcs. The palanquin was fully enclosed with glazed windows and was large enough to sport two full size lounge chairs, a small cabinet for food and drink and a wash basin.

The two Fair-Folk leaders were traveling to a human fishing village called Portnew some six miles from the main Fair-Folk encampment. Scouts had confirmed that the village held about three hundred humans and Ammon had decided that this would be the Fair-Folks first official introduction to the human race.

He had initially decided that he would set out with Seth and himself together with a minimal guard. Perhaps ten battle orcs. However, after two battle groups had come across a couple of human warriors who had killed most of them before succumbing, Ammon had decided that caution would be the better part of valor. After all, he reasoned, what if they came across ten human warriors? So he had formed up a guard consisting of five hundred battle orcs and four hundred goblin archers. Wherever they were going, they were going in strength.

'Right,' he shouted. 'Let's move out.'

The eight orcs picked up the palanquin and the rest of the guard formed up around it. Then they marched off.

'So,' said Seth. 'How do you want to play this?'

'Truthfully,' replied Ammon. 'We tell them were we are from and why we came. We tell them that we come in friendship and have no plans to conquer.'

'So semi-truthful, you mean.'

Ammon chuckled. 'Semi-truthful, truthful. Semantics my dear mage. After all we do not seek full scale war, we simply seek domination, as is our right as superior beings.'

Seth nodded. 'Truly do you speak, commander.'

'Now, when we meet, remember to glamour them. As your research has shown, we need them to see us as tall, human, attractive and powerful in an avuncular way.'

'Of course, Ammon. Consider it done.'

***

Tremain sprinted down the path into the village, chest heaving as he sucked air in. He stopped in front of squire Blamey's house and banged frantically on the door.

'Squire,' he yelled. 'It's me. Tremain. Come quickly, sir.'

There was the sound of running footsteps from within and the door was flung open. A large older man with cropped gray hair and a chest-long gray beard stood in the doorway.

'Well, what is it, young Tremain,' the man said. 'Speak to me.'

'People approaching, squire. Thousands of them. Well, not people. Things. Things are coming, squire. Monsters. Thousands of big ugly monster things. I saw them from my lookout post. They're coming down the valley towards the village. They've got swords and bows and arrows and they're all really, really ugly.'

'Calm down, boy,' snapped the squire. 'Now, take a deep breath and start again. How many are there?'

Tremain thought for a while his brow wrinkled in concentration. 'About a thousand.'

'Good. Now, you say that they are armed?'

Tremain nodded.

'How close?'

'Twenty minutes away,' answered Tremain. 'No more.'

'Alright,' said squire Blamey. 'Sound the alarm. Ring the church bells, quickly now.'

Tremain sprinted off and, just over a minute later, the peals of the church bells started rolling across the village.

The reaction was instantaneous. People ran from their houses into the street. Windows were thrown open. Five men pulling a huge wagon came into view. They pulled the wagon across the beginning of the main street into the village and then turned it onto its side to create a barrier. Since the pulses had started there had been numerous attacks from roving bands and the village was now well ready for defending themselves.

All available villagers were out in the main street. Fortunately it was the only way into the village apart from access from the sea. A perfect defensive position. Although probably not against a thousand armed warriors. However, squire Blamey was more than a little skeptical about Tremain's estimation regarding the numbers.

By now the bell had stopped ringing and the villagers stood in relative silence. There were around two hundred of them. There were more who lived in the village but they were all out fishing. It was the fishing that had enabled this village to survive the pulse so well. A hardy bunch that relied little on modernity's such as televisions and microwave ovens, they had simply converted their fishing vessels to sail power, reverted to the old ways of fish oil lamps and cooking over fires and life continued as before. Missus Johnston had been lost to her diabetes and old Bobby Holmes had died from a heart attack but apart from those two casualties, the village was as strong as ever.

And now they waited for their next trial. All of them were armed, after a fashion. A smattering of shotguns, billhooks, cleavers, spears and pitchforks. Even the odd sword.

They could hear the interlopers approaching, still hidden from view by the undulations in the road. But their marching footsteps were getting closer and closer. And, as they broached the hill, squire Blamey saw that Tremain had not been exaggerating. There were at least a thousand of them. And they were monsters. Broad gray, pig faced monstrosities. Piggy little eyes, holes instead of ears and nostrils of flapping skin. Behind them a horde of grossly misshapen creatures. Short with arms so long that they almost dragged on the ground. Massive pectoral and arm muscles that were totally out of proportion to their short bandy legs.

There was a collective gasp from the crowd but, to squire Blamey's pride, no one stepped back or left their position. They were Cornish men and women. Tough and proud.

The horde of monsters came to a halt a mere twenty yards from the wagon barrier, crashing their feet down in unison as they did so. Then the ranks parted and eight of them walked forward, they were carrying an enclosed palanquin that they lowered carefully to the ground.

One of the orcs opened the door to the palanquin and stood back.

And from it stepped two men. Both stood at over six foot. They wore pants of brown suede leather, knee high boots and white, loose fitting cotton shirts. Both had long golden blond hair although one had it tied up in a ponytail. Their features were perfect. Chiselled with high cheekbones, masculine chins and deep blue eyes. Their hips narrow and their shoulders broad. They seemed to exude an almost palpable aura of power. There was a collective gasp from the crowd.

Squire Blamey looked on the two men and felt small. Dirty and worthless. And then they smiled at him and all was good as he felt their approval, their concern for his feelings, their empathy.

The two stepped forward.

'We would like to speak to your leader,' said the one without the ponytail.

Squire Blamey stepped forward. 'Well, that would be me then.'

And the two Fair-Folk covered him with their golden presence.

Chapter 5

Nathaniel had spent another three days in the village. During that time the villagers and the soldiers had hammered together a committee that seemed like it would suit all involved. Houses had been repatriated, the kitchens had been combined and work was handed out on a more equitable basis. Also, the training of the children now included math, history, English and general studies.

It was a working model and, bar any freakish acts-of-god Nathaniel was sure that the village would survive and prosper in the years to come.

He left early on the morning of the forth day. Before sunrise. Without saying goodbye. Leaving only his legacy behind.

As was his custom he continued to travel in a vaguely northerly direction. Following rivers when he could as they provided both water and more edible plant life.

He met a small band of people after a week or so. Family based. Father, mother, six children, uncles, aunties. They had raised a small tent hamlet next to the river and built a crude wooden stockade around it.

They were very wary of the marine but welcomed him into their enclave. There was no way that they could have stopped him, even if they had wanted to.

Nathaniel gave them three rabbits, some wild carrots and potatoes and they made a fish stew. They also shared some of their poteen, a distilled white alcohol made from vegetable peelings. It smelled like paint stripper and tasted worse. But Nathaniel accepted his ration with grace. They didn't talk much. It was as if there was nothing in the world left to talk about. They were alive. Many were dead. They would continue to exist until they died. And that was it.

The marine left early the next morning feeling profoundly depressed. There were so few people left and the die back was continuing. As the winter became harsher he knew that it would claim many more lives. The family unit that he had just left would find it harder to fish as the river froze over. Edible plants and roots would be impossible to find under the snow and game would become scarcer. The weakest would go first. Probably the youngest of the children and the oldest adults. Unless they kept fires going constantly the cold would eventually kill them all, as their bodies grew weaker and less able to combat the effects of the low temperatures.

Nathaniel's thoughts became more and more morbid as he imagined himself one of only a handful of people left alive on a frozen island. Wandering in solitude like the great blue whales, their population so decimated that they could not even find each other to mate.

It was in this mood, after a few hours of riding, that he came upon the fence. A high, chain link affair with a curved top. However, the top was curved inwards in order to stop people escaping. But the fence itself was too lightweight to be a prison fence. And there were no guard towers.

Intrigued, Nathaniel decided to follow it and see what it was. He randomly chose to go right and, after around five minutes, he came across a high steel gate. On the gate was a sign, 'Barnet House Psychiatric Hospital'. That explained the fence.

His curiosity assuaged, the marine decided to press on. He had no desire to visit a lunatic asylum and he already had sufficient supplies of food so there was no real need.

He nudged his horse with his heels and it broke into a faster walk, following the fence line, hooves crunching in the crisp snow.

The horse heard the noise just before Nathaniel and it stopped walking and pricked it's ears up. The marine wasn't sure what it was. Almost the sound of wind. Maybe a keening animal. Nathaniel cocked his head to one side and concentrated. It was coming from a copse of fir trees on his left. He drew one of his shotguns and nudged the horse forward. As he got closer to the sound it became more obviously human. He dismounted and walked forward, pushing into the thick growth.

There, sitting naked in the snow, was an adult man. His hair long and stringy with grease and dirt, his skin blue with cold. He had a pile of wood in front of him and was rubbing two sticks together in a completely unsuccessful attempt to start a fire.

And all the while he keened like a trapped animal.

He looked up at Nathaniel as the marine approached. 'Good day, sire,' he said. His voice a loud stage whisper. Both sibilant and demanding at once. 'Welcome to my house. Please close the door, you'll let all the heat out.' He continued rubbing the sticks together.

'So, my liege,' he continued. 'Pray be seated. Won't be long and we shall have a nice steaming bowl of stew to nourish us. Oh yes. Stew. Beef. Not pork. No, no,' he mumbled to himself as he shook his head vehemently. 'Never pork. Never ever.'

Nathaniel went back to his horse and pulled a fur blanket from, his saddlebag. He came back and draped it around the naked man's shoulders.

The man looked puzzled. Then he stroked the fur. 'Soft,' he said. 'Warm.'

Nathaniel nodded, then asked. 'What is your name?'

The man shook his head. 'Don't know. Funny that, I know that I have a name. I know that. But can't remember it, sire. Can't remember.' He stared at the pile of wood for a while and then tears rolled down his cheeks. 'No fire,' he said. 'And no stew. None. Not even pork. Nasty pork.'

'Are you from the hospital?' Asked Nathaniel.

'Yes,' replied the man. 'I suppose that I am. I'm mad, you see, my liege. Mad. But I had to leave, had to. Pork stew. Nasty. Had to leave.'

'Are you Jewish?' Asked Nathaniel, wondering at the man's aversion to pork.

The man glanced down at his own penis and pulled at it, displaying his foreskin. 'No, see. Not Jewish. No, no. Pork is evil. Evil.'

'Well you can't stay out here,' aid Nathaniel. 'You'll die. I need to take you back.'

The man nodded. 'No escape. Must go back. Mad, completely mad.'

Nathaniel led the man to his horse and helped him mount up. Then the marine led the horse back to the gates. But the gates were locked and there was no way in.

'How did you get out?' He asked the man.

'Climbed a tree,' he said. 'Jumped. Flew. Like a squirrel. Flew and flew.'

Nathaniel thought for a while. Then he drew one of his shotguns out. 'Block you ears,' he said to the man. The man clasped his hands over his ears like a child. Nathaniel pulled the trigger twice. Then he flipped open the shotgun, reloaded and fired twice again. Then they waited.

They didn't have to wait that long before a man in a thick woollen coat came trudging down the long driveway towards them.

'Hello,' he shouted as he drew near.

'Hello,' greeted Nathaniel in return.

'Ah, I see that you have found mister Cosmo for us.'

The naked man nodded. 'That's right. Cosmo. He knows. He knows. I be Cosmo, sire. Cosmo, the not Jew, esquire. Mad. At your service, my liege.'

'My name is doctor Luckman, Henry Luckman,' said the newcomer as he pulled a bunch of keys from his pocket. 'I'm the head doctor at this establishment.' He unlocked the gate, opened it and beckoned to them to come in, closing the gate behind them.

Nathaniel continued to lead the horse as he followed the doctor up the driveway.

'Thank you very much for bringing Cosmo back,' said the doctor. 'Mister?'

'Hogan. Master sergeant Nathaniel Hogan, United States Marine Corps.'

'Impressive, 'said doctor Luckman. 'And what brings you to these parts?'

'I was based in London. At the embassy. Left. Headed north. That's about it.'

They reached the front door of the hospital. It was a large Victorian edifice done in a Gothic revival style. All red brick, mullioned windows, cupolas and round roof turrets.

'Tie your horse up here to the railings,' said Luckman. 'I'll send someone to take care of it. Come inside and let's get Cosmo warm and dressed.'

The interior of the building was dark and cold. The double volume entrance hall so gloomy that the ceiling was hidden in darkness.

They traipsed down a dingy corridor past rows of doors until they came to room number 47. The doctor opened the door and steered Cosmo in.

The room was tiny. A single steel bed, thin mattress, scratchy grey and blue blanket. A grimy window let in a shaft of dirty light. Dust motes danced in the dull beam. The room smelled of mildew and stale urine. Sour and musty.

Nathaniel noticed that the bed had side rails with leather retaining straps attached.

Doctor Luckman helped the inmate into a tracksuit. A faded yellow nylon with black stripes down the arms. The color brought out the unhealthy pallor of Cosmo's complexion. Sallow spongy flesh and red-rimmed eyes.

He sat down on the bed, hands between his knees, face blank.

Luckman and Nathaniel left the room. The doctor locked the door behind them.

'What's wrong with him?' Asked Nathaniel.

'Delusions,' answered Luckman. 'Combined with paraphrenia and late onset psychosis. The whole package.'

'What can you do for him?'

'Not much, sergeant. We have been administering respiridone but our stocks of most drugs have now run out. We try to keep them safe. Alive. Therapy when we can. There are over one hundred and twenty patients and only six staff. Myself, doctor Maxim, four nurses. Three male and one female. The rest left to try to reach their families. None returned.'

'How are you for supplies? Food, water?'

A stream runs past the north fence. And we have some livestock. Sheep and pigs. At the moment we are fine. Well off, actually. Please, stay with us for the night if you'd like. Rest up and get some food inside you. There's lots of extra room.'

Nathaniel nodded. 'Thank you, doctor. I will.'

The doctor showed Nathaniel to a room on the second floor of the institute. It was substantially larger than Cosmo's room and it had the added luxury of a fireplace. A small stack of logs and kindling stood next to the fireplace and the bed had a bright red woolen blanket on it.

'I'll get someone to bring your kit up and to stable your horse,' said Luckman. 'I'm afraid that I must ask that you stay in your room unless someone comes to escort you. We do have some patients who tend to wander and they can be dangerous. Also, the sight of a stranger may cause some of them to panic. I hope that you don't mind?'

Nathaniel shook his head. 'Not at all. I'll use the chance to get some rest. Thanks, doctor. I appreciate the welcome.'

Luckman smiled and left the room. Nathaniel heard the key turn and when he tried the doorknob he found that the room had been locked. He thought it a little strange but was unperturbed. If he did feel the need to go anywhere he could walk through the locked door as easy as if it were made of cardboard.

He went to the bed, stripped back the blanket and went to sleep.

***

Nathaniel woke to the sound of the doorknob turning. He slipped out of bed and stood against the wall. He glanced out of the window and was surprised to see that it was already dark. He had slept for at least four hours.

Doctor Luckman walked into the room holding a lit candle.

'Sergeant,' he whispered.

'Over here,' answered Nathaniel.

Luckman literally jumped a foot into the air. 'Holy crap! You shocked me.'

Nathaniel grinned. 'Sorry, doc.'

'I was wondering if you would like to join the staff for an early meal. We tend to eat when the sun goes down and wake with it's rising.'

The marine nodded. Thank you, doctor. Should I follow you?'

'Please.'

Luckman turned from the room and led Nathaniel down the corridor. They descended a flight of stairs and then meandered through a maze of corridors, the candle the only light to guide them. Some of the rooms that they passed had their doors shut but it was obvious from the moans and groans inside that they housed patients.

'Are any of the patients dangerous?' Asked Nathaniel.

The doctor shook his head. 'Only to themselves. Or perhaps they may inadvertently strike out, but we have no psychopaths or such what. Although, I am sure that the main reason that we have not been disturbed or even attacked by any roving gangs is that people assume that the place is overrun with madmen. What with the high fence and all, people assume the worst. All the better for our security. Ah, here we are. 'Luckman pushed open a door and led Nathaniel into the kitchens.

There were five people sitting around a large wooden table in the center of the kitchen. Randomly placed candles provided flickering pools of light that reflected off the stainless steel catering goods. Stoves, refrigerators and sinks. None of them working anymore. The cooking was being done on a small wood-burning stove situated under an open window, a makeshift flue guiding the bulk of the smoke out of the room.

Nathaniel could smell the food. A rich stew of some sort. His mouth instantly started watering as he realized how hungry he was.

Luckman introduced everyone as a group.

'People,' he said. 'This is sergeant Nathaniel Hogan. Sergeant, these are the doctors and nurses that I told you about.'

The people at the table mumbled a response, their demeanor less than friendly.

There were four men and a person wearing a dress. Nathaniel assumed that she was a woman although the large quantity of hair on her upper lip and her massive, raw-boned hands tried desperately to belie the fact. The woman stood up, walked over to the stove and lifted the lid off the pot. She gave the stew a perfunctory stir and then grunted her approval. She ladled two plates full and brought them back to the table, placing one in front of the doctor and one in front of the marine. Nathaniel thanked her but she completely ignored him. She shuttled back and forth two more times, serving everyone. Then she went around the table pouring water from a jug into glasses. Once again Nathaniel voiced his thanks and once again she ignored him as if he didn't exist.

The stew was good. Rich and high on meat and fat. Barely any vegetables. It suited Nathaniel who had been living on a diet of lean rabbit and root vegetables. Apart from Luckman, who kept up an uninterrupted patter, the rest of the table said nothing. The only other sound beside Luckman's chatter was the slurping and grunting of the woman as she snuffled away at her plate of food. She fetched herself two more helpings before Nathaniel had even finished one.

'The first few weeks were the easiest,' said Luckman. 'We had all of the necessary drugs and more staff than we do now. But, by the end of the second week we were out of most of the stronger drugs and people had accepted that the lights weren't coming back on, so most of them left to find their families and such. We all stayed on. Someone had to. Many of the patients are almost comatose. Some show dangerous levels of self-violence. Most of them have to be restrained for their own safety. And now, with the drugs all gone, we are starting to experiment with more old fashioned methods.'

'Like what?' Asked Nathaniel.

'Acupuncture. Art therapy. Hypnotism.'

'Does it work?'

Luckman shrugged. 'Not really. Sometimes a little.'

The woman spoke for the first time. Her voice was surprisingly high and breathless. Like a small child. She even had a slight lisp. 'Discipline,' she said. 'Discipline, a bland diet and lots of fresh air. Sometimes the old ways can be the best.'

'What do you mean?' Asked Nathaniel. 'Do you mean like beatings and starvation?'

She nodded. 'If needs be. It's for their own good you know. They need to stay docile or else how could we control so many of them. Without us they wouldn't last a week. Not even three days and some would be dying from lack of water. Many of them are incapable of even the simplest of tasks.'

She snuffled as she shoveled more stew into her mouth, chewing noisily. Mouth open.

The rest of the table stood up and took their dishes to the sink. Nathaniel did the same. The woman had taken the pot of stew to the table and was scraping the remnants onto her plate, licking her lips noisily as she did so.

Nathaniel looked away. The sight of her made him feel nauseous and the pig-like sounds that she made didn't help very much.

'Doctor Luckman,' said Nathaniel. 'I know that it's early but I'd like to take this chance to catch up on my sleep and then leave real early if that's okay by you?'

'Of course, sergeant,' agreed Luckman. 'I'll escort you to your room.'

'No need,' said Nathaniel. 'I know the way.'

'On no, that won't do,' fussed Luckman. 'After all, there is your safety to think about as well as the safety of the patients.'

Nathaniel thought about arguing and then decided that he just couldn't be bothered. A good nights sleep and then he was out of here.

Once again they trudged through dark, dank corridors until they came to Nathaniel's room. The doctor gave Nathaniel a lit candle, closed the door and locked it.

With a skill brought from years of military training the marine lay down and fell asleep almost immediately, sticking to the old maxim of sleep and eat whenever you can, because tomorrow you may not get the chance.

The next morning he awoke early, perhaps two hours before sunrise. He waited for a while, sitting on the edge of his bed. Then he finally lost his patience. He put on his kit, strapped on his weapons and gave the door a shove. He felt the lock strain against the doorjamb. Trying to cause as little damage as possible, Nathaniel leant against the door and slowly applied more and more pressure. With an almost gentle pop the lock sprung and the door opened.

Now, firstly he had to get to Cosmo's room because he still had one of Nathaniel's fur blankets. Then he needed to find his horse, get someone to open the gates and go on his way.

He remembered that Cosmo had been taken to room number 47, so it was a simple task to follow the numbers until he found himself outside the room. He tried the door and, to his surprise, it was open. He walked in to find the room empty. His fur blanket was lying on the floor next to the bed. Nathaniel picked up, rolled and slung it over his shoulder.

Next to find where his horse was.

He wandered aimlessly along the dark corridors. He could hear patients behind locked doors. Some weeping, some shouting, others carrying on what seemed like a totally normal conversation, bar the fact that they were alone.

He quickly lost his bearings in the Escher-like meanderings of the Gothic build. Some corridors simply petered out. Others took a bewildering series of turns. Some rose up a series of steps and then dropped by the same number again. Some almost pitch black. At one stage he contemplated taking out his axe and simply hewing a straight line from where he was to an exterior wall.

Finally he heard a noise. Two voices talking. One high, one low. Luckman and the female nurse with the appetite. He headed down the corridor towards the door at the end that had light flowing from under it.

He turned the door handle.

And entered hell.

Cosmo's body hung suspended from a butcher's hook in the center of the room. Hundreds of candles lit the area with a bright orange firelight. Hellfire. Luckman and the nurse wore long green surgical aprons. Both carried meat cleavers.

Cosmo's throat had been cut and he had been eviscerated. Nathaniel noticed his entrails sitting in a bucket close to his feet. They had started to flay the body, peeling the skin off, starting at his shoulders and working down. Red wet flesh exposed to the blaze of the myriad candles.

In the far corner of the room were more butchers hooks hanging from the ceiling. Each one held a large portion of dressed red meat. Human flesh. Prepared for consumption.

In the days of old, people used to refer to it as "long pork".

Nathaniel suddenly understood Cosmo's obsessive hatred of pork.

The woman screwed her face up and ran at the marine, her cleaver held above her head. Nathaniel simply whipped out a straight left jab that caught her flush on her nose, smashing it flat as it knocked her to the floor. She thrashed around on the tiled floor, slipping and sliding in the blood and squealing in a high porcine fashion. Grunting and slobbering at the same time.

Luckman didn't move. Simply stood, with a wry smile on his face. Seemingly unperturbed.

'You said that you had cattle,' said Nathaniel. 'Cows and sheep and pigs.'

Luckman shrugged. 'Sorry. I lied. What did you expect? Hi, stranger, we're doing fine for food because we eat the patients. Get real.'

Nathaniel felt bile rise in his throat as he remembered the stew from the night before. Rich and flavorful. Slightly fatty. The room spun around him and he forced his head back into the game.

'You can't eat people,' he said.

'Why not?'

'I…because. It's evil.'

'Says who?'

'Look,' continued Nathaniel. 'You just can't. No argument, end of story.'

'I see,' said Luckman. 'So you are now the judge and jury of all that you see. In a world gone mad you are the only sane one left. The guardian. What gives you the right? Stuff you very much, marine master sergeant. Stuff you utterly and completely. A couple of shotguns and a big axe do not give you the right to decide the path of the new world. We do what we have to do to stay alive. No more and no less. We are not killing for pleasure. We kill for survival. Without us many of these patients would die lingering horrible deaths. With us, at least they are kept as comfortable as possible and, in the end, their death is swift and they help others to live. We give their lives meaning. Who are you to take that away, you self righteous prick?'

On the floor the fat nurse giggled. 'Prick,' she snorted. 'Prick, prick, prick.'

Nathaniel stood for a while. The strength of his emotions battered away at him like a gale. He could feel the storm picking at his riggings, threatening to tear away his anchor. His very humanity.

Eventually he spoke.

'Where is my horse?'

'If you go back down this corridor. Turn left at the stairway at the end. Follow it up until you get to a door. The door leads outside. The stables are at the back.'

'What about the gates?'

Luckman put his hand in his pocket, drew out a large key and threw it to Nathaniel who caught it.

'Lock the gate behind you. Throw the key back in.'

Nathaniel walked backwards to the door, opened it.

'Sergeant,' said Luckman. 'Good luck. I mean it.'

The marine stared at the doctor for a while.

'Go to hell, doctor. I mean it too.'

And Nathaniel left the building.

It had been two weeks since commander Ammon and mage Seth had gone to the fishing village of Portnew to introduce themselves to the humans. And the meeting had been very prosperous. Ammon had set up a trading agreement with the village. In return for fish, fish oil and samphire edible seaweeds, Ammon had agreed to leave a contingent of battle orcs and goblins to protect the villagers from attack by roving groups of bandits. Two hundred orcs and one hundred goblins archers had been left behind with instructions to build a fortified stockade across the only entrance to the village. This would include large gates that would be constantly manned.

Ostensibly, the Fair-Folk now controlled access both in and out of Portnew. And they were being rewarded for the privilege.

Commander Ammon had wasted no time. As soon as he and Seth had returned to the Fair-Folk encampment he had put together another twenty bands of emissaries, each complete with their own contingent of battle orcs and goblins. They were all furnished with the same task. Do the same as Ammon had done to Portnew.

Within ten days the Fair-Folk had struck up similar agreements with another twenty-two towns and villages stretching from Coverack in the south to Polzeath in the north of the county.

Each one of these places had a minimum of two hundred battle orcs and one hundred goblins. Some of the larger establishments, had as many as five hundred orcs. Supplementing these permanent forts, Ammon had also arranged another twenty sets of fast battle groups, one hundred orcs and fifty goblins each, to patrol between the towns and villages on a constant rotational basis, checking on command structures, relaying messages and bringing intel back to Ammon.

To all intents and purposes, Cornwall was now under the control of the Fair-Folk.

***

Donal Treago was the eldest of nine brothers. Their ma wasn't Catholic or anything. She simply enjoyed having children. Although, in all fairness, she had said that the last three boys were her attempt to have a daughter. She never did produce a female of the line and died giving birth to Jamie, younger than Donal by some twenty years.

When the pulse had hit, Donal had gathered the clan, including all of the relatives from the Bescoby side of the family. All told, including women and children, there were over one hundred and thirty of them. Sixty men and teenagers of near adult size and capability.

Between the entire clan they owned a substantial swath of land in central Cornwall. More than enough to subsist on. However, the unseasonable winter had taken its toll on both their crops and their livestock and they had been driven to hunt. And not only for game. They had also turned to raiding small hamlets and villages. Fishing villages were the most profitable as they often had an abundance of both fresh and dried fish, a great source of protein.

It had been over two weeks since the last raid and it was time. The clan had gathered and Donal had decided that they would march to Tryree, a fishing village on the west coast of Cornwall, some twelve miles from the

Treago farm. As always, their plan was simplicity itself. Every adult capable of fighting would be armed with either shotguns or hunting rifles. They would simply advance, en masse, towards the village. Threats would be made and dissenters would be shot. Then they would strip the village of food and leave.

The first part of the plan went well. The march was uneventful.

But when the clan arrived at the village they found that the only entrance was blocked by a six-foot high wooden stockade. Built into the stockade was a sturdy double gate and, on each side of the gate a ten-foot tower. There appeared to be no defenders on the wall itself, or on the towers.

After a brief confabulation, Donal and ten men approached the gates. They walked up, weapons at the ready. When they were ten feet from the gates they stopped and Donal called out.

'Hey! Open the gates. We mean no harm. We have come to trade.'

After less than a minute the gate creaked open and something stepped out.

There was a collective intake of breath.

'What they hell?' Expressed Donal.

In front of them was an armor clad being. Perhaps five foot ten, dressed in full battle armor but without a helmet, holding a broadsword and buckler.

And it was not human. Grey, rubber-like skin. No nose or ears. Deep set black eyes. Massive claws on the end of each finger.

The thing cast its gaze over the clan.

'You have not come in peace,' the thing rumbled. 'You are obviously a party of war. Where are your wagons, your women folk, children?'

'We left them at home,' shouted Donal. 'Now let us in, you pig ugly monster, or I swear, there will be hell to pay.'

The creature tilted its head to one side, thinking. Then it spoke again.

'Go away or we will kill you all. I have spoken. Now obey or die.'

The thing turned its back on the clan and walked back into the gate. As it did so, Donal raised his shotgun and fired. A volley of pellets struck the creature's back. Some pellets bounced off the armor, some penetrated its flesh.

Immediately the air was filled with a sound like a huge flock of birds taking wing and a shadow passed over the sun. The clan looked up to see a cloud of over one hundred yard-long steel tipped arrows arcing through the sky towards them.

'Oh crap,' said Donal as he looked up. 'Run!'

Before the first volley had even struck, the second had been launched. And then the third as the goblin archers did what they did best.

The sound of steel striking flesh thudded across the land as the clan was stuck down by the hail of missiles.

And then the gates were flung open and the battle orcs poured forth, ululating and screaming as they came.

To call it a battle would be vastly exaggerating things. It was a mere slaughter. Eight minutes of broadswords cleaving human flesh. Eight minutes of screaming and pleading and agony. Eight minutes of death.

And then silence.

The orcs had defended the village. A pact had been sealed. They were now, truly, allies.

From the village the cheers of the thin skins could be heard as they sang their praises of the Fair-Folk's soldiers.

Chapter 7

The Jesuits say, give me a child at seven and I shall show you the adult. If that saying is true then Emily Thomas, Milly to her friends, was going to grow up to be forthright, confident, caring and inquisitive.

If she was going to grow up at all. And, at the moment, that did not look probable.

There were three bad men. One stood over her. He had open sores all over his face and his breath smelt of rotten meat. It made Milly's tummy feel sick. The two other bad men stood over her parents. Both her mother and father lay on the floor. The men hadn't bothered to tie them up. They hadn't even knocked them to the floor.

The fact was that both of her parents were on the very edge of starving to death, their bodies as drawn and emaciated as concentration camp victims. Milly was still relatively healthy. This was because her parents had ensured that she was fed and watered first. To the point that they had ensured their own starvation. It was the only way that they were able to keep their seven-year-old daughter alive.

The men had already ransacked the house and found no food. Runny sore man had kicked her daddy a few times and then had come to stand over her.

Eventually he spoke.

'You can have the old one,' he said to the two other men. 'I'm gonna do the little one.'

'No ways,' said one of the other men. 'This scrawny old bitch is almost dead. I ain't into doing dead people. I'll wait my turn with the girl. I'm a patient man.'

The third man giggled and kicked her daddy again. 'I'll do the old bird. Reckon she'll stay alive long enough. Ain't fussy. It's been a while.'

Runny sore man undid his belt and dropped his trousers to the floor.

Then he made a strange noise. A grunt. Like someone had punched him in the stomach. He sank to his knees and then, ever so slowly, his head literally rolled off his neck and fell onto the floor.

Blood squirted high and Milly screamed.

Standing behind the runny sore man was another man. Tall with black hair and emerald green eyes. In his right hand he held an axe. His face was pale with anger, his jaw muscles taut. Without saying anything he swung right, whipping the axe in a semi-circle, level to the ground. It cleaved through the giggling man's neck, causing his head to leap from his shoulders. Without pause the axe twisted and returned, striking the third man on his upper arm and lopping it off. The deadly blade continued its journey of death and clove through the man's body, smashing ribs and muscles and cartilage as it hewed him in half.

The big man wiped the axe one of the dead men's shirts and clipped it back onto his belt. Then he knelt down next to Milly. When he spoke his voice was quiet. Gentle. Caring.

'Please don't be afraid,' he said. 'I am your friend. I am here to help. Trust me. Did they hurt you?'

Milly shook her head.

'Good,' said the man as he stood up and walked over to her mommy and daddy.

He knelt next to them. First he checked her daddy, holding his hand against her daddy's neck for a while. He shook his head to himself and then did the same to her mommy. He nodded and took a canteen of water from his webbing. Opened it. Held her mommy's head up and trickled water into her desiccated mouth.

Most of it dribbled out but he was patient. Patient and tender. And eventually she started to swallow. After a few minutes her eyelids fluttered and she stared up at the big man, slowly coming into focus.

'My baby?' She croaked.

'She's safe,' said Nathaniel.

The little girl came over and took her mother's hand.

The mother smiled.

'Take care of her,' she said to Nathaniel.

The marine nodded. 'I will.'

She smiled. And, slowly, the light drained from her eyes, turning the windows to her soul into mere dead baubles.

'Mommy?'

Nathaniel picked up the girl and held her tight.

'I'm sorry, my darling,' he said. 'Your mommy and your daddy are gone. They're in heaven now, with God.'

Milly started to cry. 'No. I want God to give them back. It's not fair. Make him give them back.'

Nathaniel patted her back and held her until the tears stopped.

'What's your name, sweetheart?' He asked.

'Milly.'

'Nice name. Okay, Milly. I'm going to put you down, then we need to go outside. I am going to dig a grave for your parents. I want you to collect as many flowers as you can. Okay?'

Milly nodded.

'Good girl. Come now.'

Nathaniel dug the grave deep and he laid the couple down together. Milly insisted that he get a couple of pillows from the bedroom to lie under their heads. After he filled the hole in, Milly scattered the flowers over it. There weren't many due to the cold. Mainly the muted pinks and yellows of flowering shrubs.

'Would you like to say a prayer?' Asked Nathaniel.

Milly nodded.

'Our father, who art in heaven, Harold be thy name. Umm…forgive us our tesspass…passer. And deliver us our evil. Amen.'

'Amen,' said Nathaniel. 'That was very nice, Milly. Well done.'

He led her to his horse and lifted her up onto the saddle. Then he climbed up behind her and kicked the horse into a walk.

'What's the horse's name?' Asked Milly.

'I don't know,' said Nathaniel. 'I've never asked him.'

'That's silly. Horses can't talk. You have to name him.'

'Okay then, Milly. Give him a name.'

'Tintin.'

'You sure?'

'Yes,' said Milly. 'Tintin.'

'Tintin it is then.'

'And what's your name?'

'I'm Nathaniel. Nathaniel Hogan.'

'That's quite a long name,' said Milly. 'I think that I will call you Nate.'

'Nate?'

'Yes.'

Nathaniel shrugged. 'Whatever.'

They rode on in silence. After a while Nathaniel realized that Milly had fallen asleep. He held her tight and they continued on their way.

He had left the asylum four days ago and had only lucked across Milly's predators because he had heard the men as they were ransacking the house. He would have left them to it but, at the last moment decided to take a look into the house. Just in case.

And now he had a young girl to take care of.

He made camp early, guiding the horse, Tintin, into the forest and picking a spot with his usual care. Sheltered from the weather, out of direct line of site of any trails.

He nudged Milly awake.

'Hey, little one. Time to get off. We make camp here.'

He dismounted and lifted Milly down.

'You collect as much wood as you can, Milly. But don't go too far. Make sure that you can still see me at all times, okay?'

Milly nodded and started to pick up kindling.

As was Nathaniel's custom, he built up three walls with snow, laid down his tarpaulin, laid the furs on top and then stretched the second tarp over the structure to form a low roof.

Then he went to his saddle bag and dug out a brace of pigeon that he had caught and plucked that morning. Milly had made a good-sized pile of wood near the front of the bivouac and Nathaniel built a small fire. He put a cast iron pot on the flames and threw in some snow to melt. As soon as the snow had become water he put a couple of handfuls of nettle leaves and sliced burdock roots in and then chucked the pigeons on top.

Next he got up and went searching for a birch tree. He found a good specimen not far from the camp and, taking his sharp knife, drilled a hole in the trunk. Then he placed a mug on the ground and fashioned a small run off using a piece of bark, draining the tree sap into the mug. Whilst the sap was draining he took the time to set up a few rabbit snares.

It didn't take long to fill the mug and when he had, he plugged the hole with snow and carried the mug back to camp.

'Here,' he offered the mug to Milly.

'What is it?'

'It's a gift from the trees,' said Nathaniel. 'Taste it. It's called Fairy juice. It makes you strong.'

Milly took a cautious sip and her eyes registered her surprise.

'Wow,' she exclaimed. 'It's sweet. Like honey. Thank you, Nate.'

Nathaniel nodded. He would tap the tree again the next morning and continue to feed her the sap for as long as birch trees were available. Because, although Milly was relatively healthy, she was painfully thin and the sap was high in carbohydrates, minerals and glucose. Perfect to get some meat on her bones.

While the stew simmered on the fire, Nathaniel took one of his black mink fur blankets and, using his knife and a length of leather cord he fashioned a small cape with a hood. He carved a neck clasp from a piece of wood and a loop of cord so that the cloak could be pulled tight against the weather.

Milly watched him with interest, sipping at her mug of sap.

Nathaniel held up the cloak.

'Here, try it on.'

Milly finished her drink, put the mug down and came over. The marine slipped the cloak over her back.

She pulled it tight around her.

'Snuggly,' she said. 'So warm.' She gave the marine a kiss on the cheek. 'Thank you.'

The marine scowled. 'Yeah, well. Whatever. Let's eat.'

After the meal Nathaniel put Milly into the bivouac and spread another fur over her. She was asleep within minutes, warm and full for the first time in many weeks.

The marine sat next to the fire for a while. As was his habit he tried to conjure up a small ball of fire like the old gipsy had shown him. But it was to no avail.

Eventually, frustrated and tired he crawled into the shelter and went to sleep.

And outside the night sky roiled with silent color as the solar pulses wreaked havoc in the heavens.

Chapter 8

Tommy Tiernan was almost a head taller than the other boys, even though he was the same age as them. He held a steel pot lid in his left arm and, in his right, a two-foot long stick. He had smeared his face with river mud to make it gray in color.

'It's not fair,' whined Billy Preston. 'Why do you always get to be the orcs. I wanna be the orcs.'

'You can't be,' said Tommy. 'Orcs are big and you're just small.'

'Not so. Anyway, orcs aren't that big. They're just wide.'

'Well I'm bigger than you,' stated Tommy. 'So what I say goes.'

Billy couldn't argue with such watertight logic so he gave up.

'Okay, I'll be the goblins,' he said.

'Uh uh,' said Tommy. 'You can't be the goblins either. Orcs and goblins don't fight each other. You have to be the human raiders. So you attack me and then I kill you. Come on. Let's go.'

Billy pouted. 'This game sucks ass. I wanna be the orcs.'

'Shut up, Billy, or I'll smack you one.'

With a look of resignation Billy attacked Tommy who proceeded to chop him into imaginary pieces with his stick.

Battle Orc, sergeant Gog, watched the two human children as he stood behind the wall of the stockade. Ever since they had repelled the clan attack, the humans had treated them like heroes. Even the children emulated them in their war games.

It was a strange feeling and one that the sergeant was not entirely equipped to handle. There were no Orc children. Just as there were no Orc females. The battle Orcs were created by the Fair-Folk via a combination of both magik and arcane science. They were grown in large ceramic eggs until they reached the larval stage of development. They were then taken from the eggs and moved to the growing vats where they were suspended in a viscous protein bath. Within two months they had reached full size and their training began.

Goblins were different. They were sequential hermaphrodites. Capable of being either male or female depending on various extraneous conditions such as availability of food and water, the clemency of the weather and even social circumstances such as war. Externally, however, they continued to look the same, it was merely their personal odor that changed, allowing other goblins to know whether their male or female genitalia were in ascendancy. And their brood stocks were brought up in secret, far from the eyes of the Orcs. But Gog did know that, like the battle Orcs, the goblin brood grew to adult size very quickly. A matter of months. Then they too were sent for training, spending most of their waking moments at the archery butts while the Orcs trained with sword and shield.

Tommy looked up at sergeant Gog and waved.

Gog waved back and then wondered why he had.

He turned his back on the little thin skins and continued to scan the horizon. Looking for enemies.

Chapter 9

They had ridden slowly all day, stopping for lunch and drinks of sap that Nathaniel had tapped for Milly. Then the marine had pitched an early camp, started a fire, put some burdock roots in the coals to cook and spit roasted two rabbits that he had snared the night before.

Milly sat on a log next to the fire, her new fur cloak pulled around her. She was watching Nathaniel. Although she could see that he was a scary man, she was unafraid. She had seen his gentle side as well as his almost superhuman combat facilities. But he was distant. Troubled. Sad even.

As she was watching him she saw him slowly unclip has axe from his belt and lay it on the ground in front of him.

'Show yourself, stranger,' he called out.

Milly glanced around her but saw nothing.

'You're welcome to share the fire and get a bite to eat,' continued the marine. 'But if you continue to skulk around out there I might become suspicious of your intentions. You don't want that, trust me.'

A man stepped out of the deep shadows. A black beard and unkempt hair covered much of his face. He was carrying a long spear made from a wooden pole with a carving knife strapped on the end and wore a grey greatcoat that was slightly shiny with age, its collars and cuffs threadbare and unravelled.

'I mean no harm,' he said.

His voice was odd. A loud whisper. Like he was trying to project his voice but couldn't. When he took another step forward Milly could see why. A jagged, violent red scar ran across his throat from ear to ear. His eyes flickered from side to side like an herbivore looking for a predator. Hunted. Nervous.

Nathaniel gestured towards the fire.

'Sit.'

The man pegged the butt of the spear into the snow and sat down opposite Milly and Nathaniel. He held out his hands to the fire and eyed the rabbits hungrily.

Nathaniel took one of the rabbits off the fire, rolled it in the snow to cool it down a little and then handed it to the stranger.

'Eat.'

The man took the offering with a nod of his head and started gnawing at the meat. It was obvious that he was ravenous.

Nathaniel used a stick to pull some of the burdock roots from the coals. He skewered them and gave them to the stranger.

'Here. Eat these as well. Can't survive on rabbit unless you eat something else with it. Body can't process the flesh. Not enough fat in it.'

The man blew on the roots to cool them and then chewed away.

Nathaniel cut up the second rabbit and more of the roots, put some on a plate for Milly and served her. She ate without talking as he finished off what was left.

'My name's Barnaby,' rasped the stranger. 'Barnaby Wells. Thank you kindly for the food, big man. I appreciate it, I do.'

'Nathaniel Hogan. United States Marine Corp. This here is Milly.'

Milly smiled. 'Hi.'

The stranger grunted at her.

'So where do you hail from, Barnaby?'

'I used to have a farm,' answered Barnaby. 'Some twenty miles south west of here.'

'Used to?'

'Aye. Things were all right after the sun thing happened. Had cows, sheep. A few crops. Hand pump for the well. Most of my labor was local. Five young men. Two of them married, no children. I had a wife and a daughter. The boys moved their families onto the farm. Had a nice little community going. Then the others came one night. Set fire to the farmhouse. Killed all as they tried to escape the flames. I had my shotgun. Killed two of them. They hit me on the head, cut my throat. Left me for dead. Next morning I woke up, crawled into the forest. Been running and hiding ever since.'

'I'm sorry,' said Nathaniel. 'Tough break, man. Have you seen them since?'

Barnaby shook his head. 'Don't think so. Seen some gangs. Not big enough to be them.' He put his head in his hands. 'Why did they have to kill everyone? Why can't the survivors all help each other? Why is it all so messed up?'

'It's man's default setting, Barnaby. We think that we're civilized, but inside every one of us waits a monster, simply waiting to get out. Begging to be let free to do as it will. Life is a cock up, my friend. And then you die.'

'That's not true,' cried out Milly, tears in her eyes. 'That's not true. Say so, Nate. Say it's not true.' She burst into tears.

The marine took her into his arms.

'I'm sorry, my sweet. Pay no attention. Of course it's not true,' he assured her.

But his eyes belied his words.

Eventually Milly fell asleep in Nathaniel's arms and he picked her up and put her to bed in the bivouac.

Then he went back outside and sat next to the fire. Awake.

He would not sleep with a stranger amongst them.

He would not allow any harm to come to Milly.

The fire burned low.

Barnaby curled up next to it and, grasping his makeshift spear, went to sleep.

And the Forever Man kept guard.

***

That morning Nathaniel filled a pot with Beech sap and boiled some burdock roots in it until they were soft and the liquid had reduced down to a syrupy consistency. After that he mashed the whole lot up and served. It tasted like very sweet porridge.

Then he packed up the camp, saddled Tintin, put Milly up and jumped up behind her. He delved into his saddlebag and pulled out two lengths of wire that had been attached to small wooden stakes. The wire formed a noose that stuck out from the side of the pointed piece of wood.

He handed them to Barnaby.

'Here,' he said. 'They're rabbit snares. Peg them in when you see a game trial or path. Set them, at night before you camp down. Remember, dig up burdock roots and wild carrots whenever you can. You'll starve on just rabbit.'

Barnaby took the snares. 'Thanks, marine. But can't I stay with you?'

Nathaniel shook his head. 'Sorry, dude. We travel alone.' He nudged his horse into a fast walk. 'Keep safe, stranger.'

Barnaby stood and waved at them until they were out of sight, then he sat down next to the remains of the fire and stared blankly at the snow. He ran his fingers over the wire loops and wondered what a game trail looked like.

Then he threw back his head and howled in anguish.

No one heard him.

***

It would surprise most people to know that, although the United Kingdom is a highly populated country only six percent of it is classified as urban, As well as this almost one sixth of the land mass is covered in forest.

This means that it is entirely possible to travel both the length and breadth of England without ever entering a city, town or village.

That is what Nathaniel had been attempting to do. But sometimes, although possible, it was impractical. And after all, he figured, what would be the harm in taking a short cut through a suburban area?

The marine cast his gaze over the sprawl of houses that seemed to stretch from one end of the horizon to the other. He wasn't sure exactly where he was or what city he was looking at. If he had to guess he would have said Sheffield. As it happens, it was Nottingham, but that fact would make no difference to the marine.

He nudged Tintin in the flanks and the horse walked forward. Milly pulled her cloak tight around her. They trudged slowly through one of the city's outer suburbs. A lower middle class area. Victorian terraced houses strung together. Three bedrooms, family bathroom. Guest toilet downstairs. For some reason, many of them were mere burned out shells. Some serious fire had rampaged through the neighborhood at some stage. Nathaniel judged that the conflagration had happened some three or four weeks ago, judging from the amount of snow on top of the charred hulks.

The place was deathly quiet and there was no sign of people. It was like a plague had swept the area. It puzzled the marine, as he would have expected at least a few survivors. Perhaps they were hiding.

Tintin stumbled slightly on a patch of ice that covered the tarred road so Nathaniel dismounted and helped Milly off. He figured that they could walk alongside the horse for a while. It wasn't worth risking an injury to their only mode of transport bar their own leg power.

They turned the corner into a street that was even more burned and broken down than the others they had passed. It must have been the epicenter of some major battle as Nathaniel noticed burned corpses in some of the downstairs rooms. Some of them had limbs missing. Lying on the pavement he spotted a severed arm, shriveled and desiccated. It must have been there for at least a month.

He kicked at the snow, exposing the surface below. The ground was covered with expended shotgun shells and shiny brass cartridges. The marine was starting to regret his decision to come this way and, unconsciously, he began to speed up.

He started as he heard a sound, but it was only a kitten running across the road into a service alley that ran between two houses.

Milly immediately ran after the tiny feline.

'Oh, look. Kitty,' she followed it into the service alley. 'Come, kitty.'

Nathaniel ran after her. 'No, Milly. Wait.'

He quickly tied Tintin to a street lamp and jogged into the alley that led into a patch of garden behind one of the houses.

There were four men in the garden. Nathaniel wasn't sure who was more surprised, him or them. Two of the men were holding a girl between them. Her long dark hair hung over her face but it was obvious that she had been badly beaten. Bruises and swellings stood out in livid colors against her pale skin and blood flowed from a gash in her temple.

The other two men held hunting rifles. Both were pointed at the marine. Milly stood to one side, a look of terror on her face.

Nathaniel held his hands up.

'Whoa, guys,' he said. 'I'm not here to cause trouble. Relax.'

One of the men stepped forward, his weapon still trained on Nathaniel. 'Don't tell us to relax. We'll decide if we want to relax or not. Who are you, who are you with?'

'I'm not with anyone.'

The injured girl groaned in pain.

'Is she alright?' Asked Nathaniel. 'I have a few medical supplies, maybe I should take a look at her?'

'She's fine,' said the man. 'She tried to run away and she paid the price.'

As he spoke the girl started to fit, her body shaking uncontrollably and her teeth cracking together. Blood streamed from her mouth as she bit deeply into her tongue.

'Jesus, guys,' said Nathaniel as he stepped forward. 'Put her down, let me take a look at her, please.'

'Get back,' shouted the man.

Nathaniel kept his hands up but took another step toward the fitting girl. 'I'm just going to take a look. Please, she's in trouble, man.' He took another tentative step towards her.

Without another warning the man pulled his trigger. The large hunting caliber round struck the marine in his left shoulder and spun him around. He reacted instantly, pulling his axe from his belt and swung a huge overhand blow at the man. The blade bit into his shoulder and lopped his right arm off, sending both the arm and rifle to the ground. But, as Nathaniel turned to face the others the second rifleman fired. The slug struck the marine in the center of his chest, lifted him off his feet and slammed him against the wall. The rifles barked again and the second slug hit Nathaniel in the stomach, exiting his back in a fountain of guts and gore.

He slid down the wall and collapsed on the ground as his life's blood drained into the soil.

Chapter 10

The three young men stood in front of Ammon, hands behind their backs, legs astride, eyes forward. The glamoring ensured that they saw him as all humans did. Six-foot tall, shoulder length blond hair, blue eyes. Square jawed. His build lithe and athletic. His smile kind and welcoming.

The Fair-Folk commander shook his head. 'I am sorry, good people, but we of the Fair-Folk have no need for you in our defense force. To be blunt, you have no skills that we need. Our battle orcs are superior swordsmen and our goblins are unsurpassed at their skills in archery. Perhaps you could take the place of the constructs and fetch and carry but I suspect that is not the position that you all seek.'

The youths shook their heads.

'No, sir,' said the one. 'We seek to be more involved. We want to be a part of something, an integral part, not merely a carrier of water and goods.'

'Why?' Asked Ammon.

'Well, sir, to be honest, since our world changed we do not know what to do. Before the pulse I was an apprentice electrician, now, what with no electrics, I don't know what to do. Barry here was a diesel mechanic and Vincent was a fitter and turner.'

Ammon frowned. 'I know not what these job descriptions mean. The words are foreign to me. However, I get the gist. Still, once again, I am sorry but we simply have no use for you. Now, if I were you I would be on my way. It is many hours walk to your village and you don't want to be out in the dark in this cold weather.'

Barry smiled. 'Oh no, sir,' he said. 'There's no need to worry. We came on horseback. What would be a half a day's walk is only an hour and a half on horseback. No worries, sir.'

Ammon cocked his head to one side. 'You boys come from Pennance, don't you?'

They nodded.

'Wait. We need to talk further.' Ammon put his hand to his temple and concentrated, letting his mind flow, seeking Seth.

'Yes, commander,' said the mage, his voice echoing in Ammon's mind.

'Could you come to my tent?' Pulsed Ammon back at the mage. 'We need to talk.'

'On my way,' confirmed Seth.

The mage arrived within minutes, bowing to Ammon as he entered the tent.

'How can I help, commander?'

'These youths are from the village of Pennance,' he said. 'They claim to have ridden here on horseback in an hour and one half.'

Seth nodded. 'The horse is a very fast animal, Commander,' he said. 'I have no doubt that they could have done it faster if needs be.'

'Is that true?' Asked Ammon, addressing the humans.

'Yes, sir,' said one. 'Under an hour if I wanted.'

Ammon turned to his senior mage. 'Why aren't we using these horse creatures?' He asked.

'What for, commander?'

'Many things, delivering fast messages between battle groups and villages. Emergency supplies, scouting.'

'Actually, commander,' replied Seth. 'We have tried. The horses cannot stand either the orcs nor the goblins. For some reason, when any get close to them they either bolt or attack. And when they attack they are fearsome creatures. All teeth and hooves.'

'Why don't they like us? The dogs like us.'

'Yes, sir,' agreed Seth. 'But dogs like everyone. It's in their nature. Horses are more highly strung.'

Ammon thought for a while. 'Tell me, do you have any more friends with horses?'

Vincent nodded. 'Yes, sir. Many.'

'Return in four days time. Bring another seven horse riders with you. You will officially start as scouts and messengers. We shall see where that takes us. Well done, people, and welcome to the Fair-Folk defense force.'

Chapter 11

Pain crashed through his body. A tsunami of pain, thundering across his exposed nerve endings and newly formed flesh. The pain of re-birth.

He took a deep breath and almost passed out. Stars flashed in front of his eyes and he took a moment to steady himself.

'Damn,' he growled, 'I'm going to have to stop dying before it kills me.'

The marine stood up. The first thing he noticed was that, apart from his boxers, he was naked. No shoes, no shirt, no weapons. Secondly, he was unbelievably cold. Finally, both Milly and Tintin were gone.

'Damn again,' he said as he stumbled down the alleyway and into the road.

First things first, he thought. Find some sort of clothing.

Nathaniel wandered from house to house picking up random pieces of clothing. Half a burned shirt, a pair of ragged trousers, arbitrary pieces of cloth that he simply tied around himself to keep warm. A single, bright red Doc Marten left boot in his size and, a few houses later, a black leather right foot riding boot, also in a size thirteen.

As Nathaniel left the last house he glanced at himself in a broken hall mirror.

He saw a scarecrow from hell. Burnt and bleeding. And he remembered a poem from his teenage days.

Once I said to a scarecrow, "You must be tired of standing in this lonely field."

And he said, "The joy of scaring is a deep and lasting one, and I never tire of it."

Said I, after a minute of thought, "It is true; for I too have known that joy."

Said he, "Only those who are stuffed with straw can know it."

Then I left him, not knowing whether he had complimented or belittled me.

The marine grimaced at himself.

'It's time to go scaring.'

Nathaniel had no particular plan so he decided to grid search the area until he found another living human being. The he would question them so that he could build up some intel. After that he would formulate a plan of action.

The sky was beginning to darken but the ever-present aurora overhead provided a ghostly light by which to see as it coruscated across the heavens. Blues and greens and reds. Nathaniel smelt something. He paused, sniffed the air and then simply followed his nose.

His search led him to a derelict end of terrace house. The house itself had been almost burned to the ground; all that was left was a pile of bricks, charred timber and roof tiles. However, cunningly concealed in the wreckage, Nathaniel spotted what looked like an entrance. And the smell was coming from there.

The marine delved around in the rubble, looking for a suitable weapon. Eventually he found two lengths of steel reinforcing rod, each about two feet long. He wrapped a piece of cloth around the end of each to form a handle and then he crept into the grotto.

The entrance led to a trapdoor set into the floor. Nathaniel opened it and went down the steps. There was a small room, lit by a candle and a tiny fire, a sofa and an armchair, a mattress on the floor. Many books. Above the fire were two sticks with, what appeared to be four or five rats skewered on them. They were sizzling and sputtering over the little flames. Next to the fire stood an old man. Grey bearded, a large blue overcoat, jeans and boots. In his hand he held a catering sized carving knife. His expression was wary but not scared.

'I smelt the food,' said Nathaniel. 'I mean no harm.' He dropped the two lengths of steel on the floor in front of him.

The old man gestured towards the sofa with the knife. 'Sit down, friend.'

Nathaniel sat.

'My name is Curtis,' said the old man. 'Curtis Kadogo.'

'Nathaniel. Nathaniel Hogan. Master sergeant, United States Marine Corps.'

'Welcome to my abode, jarhead,' said the old man, using the nickname for a marine soldier. 'Fancy some food?'

Nathaniel nodded. 'Thank you. I'm starving.'

The old man took a rat kebab off the fire and offered it to the marine. Then he took one himself.

Nathaniel waited for it to cool down and then took a bite. The meat was tough and rank. It filled a hole.

'Thank you.'

'Pleasure.'

The old man dipped a tin mug into a bucket of water and offered. Nathaniel downed it and handed it back. The old man helped himself to some.

'Saw you earlier,' said Curtis. 'You were dead.'

'Well,' answered Nathaniel. 'Looks can be deceiving.'

The old man shook his head. 'No. You were dead. I checked. Also you had no clothes.'

The two of them sat in silence for a while. Eventually the old man spoke again.

'So, jarhead. What gives?'

And Nathaniel told him. From the very beginning. The pulse, the embassy, the abbey, the whole immortality thing, the traveling people, the Belmarsh boys, the lunatic asylum and Milly.

The old man did not speak the whole way through and, at the end, he simply nodded and said.

'Well, that explains it then.'

'You believe me?' Asked Nathaniel.

'Yes. Only a few months back I would have reckoned that you were a few sandwiches short of a picnic, but now…the world has gone mad. I met someone last week, claimed that he had seen trolls and goblins and huge gray pig-men. Maybe he was telling the truth. Maybe not. Fact of the matter is, I never seen no pig-men but I did see you dead and now you're alive. The proof of the pudding and all that. So, I believe.'

'The men that took Milly, any idea where they might have hailed from?' Asked Nathaniel.

'Yep, got a choice of three major gangs. You got The Specials, The Overlords and The Students. Those three pretty much control the area although The Students are the big hitters.'

'The Students?'

'That's right,' said the old man. 'The Specials and The Overlords are the remnants of two drug gangs that had set up shop in the old pre-pulse Nottingham. They had weapons, structures and the will to fight. Some of the cops tried to intervene but most of them simply went home to protect their families. Can't say I blame them.

Anyway, the two drug gangs thought that they were the mean machine, but they didn't reckon on the fellows from the university. The students. It seems that the students were a few steps ahead of everyone. They figured out what the pulse was and what its effects would be in both the short and long terms. The SRC or students representative council gathered together about one hundred jocks, mainly ruby players, wrestlers and such, put a few super-bright nerds in charge of them and swung into action. There are around seven major gun stores in Nottingham and they hit every one within an hour. Rumor has it that they have an arsenal of over four thousand firearms including semi-auto assault rifles, sniper rifles and shotguns. Also around a million rounds of ammunition. Not only that, they also raided the antique arms stores and swept up all bladed weapons, crossbows, spears. Then they sent armed contingents to the three major superstores in town. They did this before the looting started, maybe three or four hours post-pulse. So now they control all of the weapons and food in the town.'

'Impressive,' admitted Nathaniel. 'So then, why are you hiding out here eating rats? Why don't you go and join the students?'

The old man laughed. 'I tried. They rejected me. Too old, they said. It's a new world order and they're strict about who they will accept. The whole thing is being run by a super-bright nutcase, goes by the rank of Senior Squire Roland. Got an IQ of over 180, Einstein stuff. Used to be a sweet kid. Problem is he suffered from paranoid schizophrenia. His meds kept it under control but now, no meds. The bastard has gone completely insane. He's like Hitler on a bad day. Thing is, he seems to be possessed of the same sort of charisma. His people worship him. Anyway, he and his cronies have put together an acceptance test. Before they let anyone in, they check age, then they make you sit an IQ test and a medical exam. I didn't get past the obvious being-an-old-man part of the interview. Stupid thing is that I worked there before this all happened. Janitor. Kept the little bastards bedrooms clean and made sure the toilets flushed. Wankers.'

'Sorry to hear that,' commiserated Nathaniel.

The old man shrugged. 'Stuff 'em. Now, your little girl. It won't be The Specials; their bit of turf is the other side of town. They wouldn't venture into The Overlords patch. So, it's either The Overlords or The Students. The Students go wherever they want and they're always out searching, particularly for youngsters that they can test and bring into the fold.'

'Where are they all situated?' Asked Nathaniel.

The Overlords are close. Two blocks north, they're in the old seaman's boarding house. Must be around fifty of them. The students are west; they've taken over the whole university campus. Four, maybe five miles away.'

'Right,' said Nathaniel. 'I'll check out The Overlords first.' He stood up. 'Thanks for the meal, old-timer. I appreciate it.'

The marine picked up his two lengths of steel rod, nodded his goodbye and left the basement.

It was dark and a light snow was falling. The wind cut through Nathaniel's rags like they weren't even there. But the ragged clothing did have its advantages. Its dark coloring and broken appearance acted like a disruptive pattern camouflage. A post apocalyptic ghillie suit and, as the marine slipped through the night, he was almost impossible to see.

He found the seaman's boarding house with ease. There were four armed guards outside the front door and a row of flaming torches made from canvas wound around wood and dipped in diesel. Keeping his distance, Nathaniel crept around the outside of the entire building, noting windows, doors, rooms with light in them and any people that he could spot. He found no conclusive proof of Milly's presence, nor could he discount it.

There was nothing else he could now do but enter the building and see if he could find the little girl.

If he was a SEAL or even an army Ranger he may have climbed onto the roof and then infiltrated through a top floor window, or found an unoccupied room and snuck in that way. But he was a marine, and by the nature of their training they approached obstacles in a much more direct fashion than any other elite forces.

Nathaniel simply erupted out of the darkness, steel reinforcing rods whipping around like helicopter blades as he mowed down the four guards. The only sound was the thud of steel on flesh and the slightly softer sound of bodies falling to the ground.

Nathaniel dropped his steel and went through the guards' weapons. Two were carrying Mac 11 submachine guns in 380 acp. Cheap crappy weapons loved by gang-bangers all over the world. Nathaniel took the 30 round magazine off the one and stuck it in the band of his trousers. He quickly stripped the weapon and threw the parts into the street, keeping the second Mac that he also pushed into his waistband. Although he now had a machine gun with 60 rounds of ammo he wasn't filled with confidence. The Mac 11 was notorious for jamming and it fired at a rate of 1200 rounds per minute. That meant that he had less than 4 seconds of fire.

The third gangster had a small 5 shot 38 revolver. Nathaniel checked that it was loaded and then stuck it into one of the rags tied around his leg. The final prostrate gangster had a double-barreled shotgun. Once again, Nathaniel checked the load and, satisfied, went up to the front door, opened it and walked in.

There was a large, empty entrance hall. A corridor ahead of him and two staircases that curved up each side of the hall to the first floor. Nathaniel reckoned that he simply needed to find someone, ask them if Milly was there and then react accordingly. A simple plan that was so simple as to not actually be a plan.

He walked slowly down the corridor, stopping outside each door and listening to see if any of the rooms were occupied. Near the end of the corridor he heard voices. He put his ear to the door. Two men talking. Maybe three.

He twisted the door handle, opened the door, stepped into the room and closed the door behind him.

He was correct. There were three men talking. However, there were also another eight men listening.

There was a split second while everyone stared at the marine who stared right back and then said.

'Crap.'

There was the terrifying sound of weapons being cocked and safety catches flicking off. And then one of the men fired. The slug missed by an inch at most and slammed into the doorframe.

Nathaniel needed no further invitation. He pulled both triggers to the shotgun, filling the room with lead pellets. Then he threw the empty weapon at the crowd, dropped to one knee, drew his Mac 11 and pulled the trigger as he swept it, right to left across the room.

There is a reason that street gangs call the Mac 11 a bullet hose. 30 rounds sprayed across the room in one and a half seconds. Using his enhanced speed, Nathaniel dropped out the expended mag, slapped in the second one and sprayed the room again. This time from left to right. Finally, he dropped the empty Mac, pulled out the little 38 and stood up, ready to question any survivors regarding Milly's whereabouts.

Unfortunately everyone was dead.

'Crap,' said the marine again.

He put the 38 back into its rag holster, quickly searched the bodies and found another three Mac 11's. He ejected their magazines, put one into his Mac and slipped the other two into his waistband.

He could hear people shouting, questioning and calling out. Footsteps thundering up and down stairs and corridors as everyone in the building dashed around attempting to find the source of the gunfire.

Sticking to his original non-plan, plan, Nathaniel simply stepped outside the room, into the corridor and waited.

Three men came running down the corridor towards him. He dispatched them with three quick bursts from the Mac. A door opened and another man ran out. The sub-machine gun burped and the man went down. Another door, another two men. The rattle of machine gun fire. Two more corpses.

Nathaniel dropped out the empty mag and slammed in another. Began to walk slowly down the corridor towards the entrance hall. He positioned himself at the bottom of the double staircase and waited. A group of men burst out from the upstairs corridor and split, half running down the one staircase and half down the other. Around twenty in total.

The marine raised the Mac, pointed at the group on the left and fired. One and a half seconds. Thirty rounds. People died. Bodies fell. Others tripped over the corpses and rolled down the stairway.

Change magazine. Point. Fire. Time edged by in microseconds as Nathaniel's gamma-enhanced speed turned mortal combat into a slow-motion movie. Another second and a half. Another thirty full metal jacketed messengers of death.

And the marine was running. Up the stairs. Pausing to pick up a pump action shotgun. He fired. Racked the pump. Fired again. Again, Again.

Blood flowed down the walls and steps as the weapon chewed into human flesh. Destroying. Disintegrating.

People fired back and bullets plucked at Nathaniel's rags. He felt a burn in his leg and glanced down to see blood flowing. Deep crimson. Staining his filthy clothing.

He drew the 38 revolver. Five shots. Two more dead. Knelt down. Picked up another shotgun. Looked around. All dead.

He ran down the corridor shouting.

'Milly! Milly! Are you there?'

More doors opened. More men died.

Finally.

Silence.

Breathing.

The odd groan of agony. Followed by a death rattle as someone's last breath shuddered from their heaving chest.

Nathaniel wandered through the building searching. But he found no one. No Milly. In fact, no women at all. Not one living soul. The Overlords were no more.

And Milly was still missing.

With heavy heart the marine collected up as much shotgun ammunition as he could find and left the building, heading for the university campus.

Heading for The Students.

Chapter 12

It was time for expansion.

The Fair-Folk now controlled the 2200 square miles that consisted of Cornwall. Ammon had set up a human cavalry detachment of one hundred riders that provided a daily messenger service between all major towns and villages. The area was no longer plagued by bandits. Food, although scarce, was available to all. For the first time since the pulse, humanity was no longer going backwards. Not in Cornwall.

Using human knowledge, Ammon had located and restarted the China clay mines of Cornwall. The clay was perfect for the manufacture of the Orc pods or eggs that were used to bring the Orcs to their larval stage of development.

The Orcs were mining vast quantities of the raw clay and groups of goblins were fashioning numerous eggs. The eggs were then fired in huge peat fed fires and then transported to either the Carnglaze caverns or the defunct Geevor tin mines where the mages initiated the initial stages of fertilization.

More Orcs were building hundreds of vast thatch roofed Longhouses that would be used to house the Orc growing vats after they had progressed to the larval stage. Like the eggs, the vats were constructed from fired clay.

At the same time, many of the goblins had morphed into the female sex due to advantageous prevailing conditions, and, very soon, they were all pregnant.

Within the next few months Ammon estimated that there would be another seven hundred thousand Orcs and goblins under his command.

With that in mind, both Ammon and Seth pored over a detailed map of the area and surrounds. Ammon stabbed at the map with his finger.

'There, there and there,' he said. 'We need full battle groups occupying Axeminster, Tiverton, South Moulton and Lynton. We also need small battle groups in every major fishing village on both the north and south side of the coast from Cornwall to Somerset. Another fifty fast battle groups patrolling the area. Each fast battle group to have at least one human horse rider, preferably two. I want our next major encampment to be built here, this side of the river outside Tiverton.'

Seth nodded. 'I agree. When and who?'

'As soon as possible. I shall send three hundred and fifty thousand battle Orcs, one two hundred and fifty thousand goblins and twenty Fair-Folk leaders. How many top mages can you spare?'

Seth thought for a while. 'I don't want to send any of the top twelve. Without the full circle, our powers diminish. However, I can send four high level wizards. Good enough for both healing and minor battle spells.'

Ammon nodded his approval. 'Do it.'

'What about constructs?' Asked the mage.

Ammon shook his head. 'I have a theory. Instead of constructs we shall call for human volunteers. They can serve, fetch and carry. Help to build. We need all of the constructs here to aid the birthing of the new Orcs and goblins.'

Seth looked doubtful. 'Why would the humans help?'

'I have no idea,' admitted Ammon. 'However, I know that they will. We have arrived at a crossroads in their development and they are looking to belong. Looking for a cause, a goal, as it were. Not all, but enough will be willing, even eager, to serve us.'

And commander Ammon was right. But, at the same time, he was wrong. Very, very wrong.

Chapter 13

Nathaniel drifted through the darkness, heading towards the university campus. It didn't take him long to walk the four miles and when he got close there was no way that he could miss the place.

The campus was surrounded by a chain link fence and the students had built ten foot high platforms every hundred yards or so. On top of each platform was what seemed to be a large parabolic mirror on a swivel with a fire grate suspended in front of it. The reflected light from the fire was concentrated by the mirror and beamed out to around one hundred yards as a bright, sodium yellow, searchlight. Nathaniel had to admit that it was pure genius. In a world without electricity The Students had constructed searchlights!

The marine stayed out of the range of the medieval searchlights and took a quick walk around the perimeter. It wasn't impenetrable but getting in would prove difficult. And, once in, there would be more guards. Nathaniel had noticed at least five groups of three, walking a beat inside the perimeter. All in all, the place looked well run and well organized. Nathaniel was mightily impressed.

He decided that the best way to get in was simply to go to the main gate and knock.

But he would do that in the morning. People were always more receptive during the hours of daylight. With that in mind he retreated back a block or so, found a hedge that butted up against a garden shed and he pushed his way under cover between the two and, using his hands as a pillow, he went to sleep.

The next morning Nathaniel rose, crept out from his cover. Then he hid his shotgun and ammunition behind the shed and set off to do another quick recce of the area.

The main gate was already open and a convoy of bicycles were leaving the campus. There must have been thirty or so, both men and women, and each bike had a trailer behind it. Accompanying the bike cavalcade were six horseman. It seemed that everyone was armed. Sidearms for the bicycle riders and rifles or shotguns for the horse guards.

It was obvious to Nathaniel that the convoy was on its way to collect something. More than likely supplies from one of the student controlled superstores in the vicinity. One again, the marine was impressed by the organization and discipline of the students.

He waited until the bikes had all gone and then he approached the gates. He walked slowly and made sure that his hands were visible. It was evident that he carried no weapons.

'Hi,' he greeted the three heavily armed guards. 'I'm looking for my niece. Small girl. Lost her yesterday. Wondering if you can help?'

The guards gave him the once over and then one stepped forward. 'You can't come in here, raggedy man,' he said. 'Only humans allowed, no scarecrows.'

The other two laughed.

Nathaniel grinned as well. 'Yeah,' he agreed. 'Good one. Lost my clothes when I lost my niece. Had to make do.'

'Turn around,' commanded the one guard.

Nathaniel did a slow 360 degree turn.

'Come on in,' said the guard. He opened the gate and ushered Nathaniel in. On the other side of the gate were three more armed guards.

'Jimmy,' said the original guard. 'Raggedy man is looking for his niece. Lost her yesterday. Wants to know if she's here. Take him to the administration block, see who's just come in.'

Jimmy nodded. 'Follow me, raggedy man.'

Nathaniel walked behind the young man. Jimmy didn't volunteer any conversation which was fine by the marine who didn't feel like talking at any rate. The campus looked almost like a standard university campus should. Groups of young adults sitting on benches, walking, talking. The only difference is that some were armed. Also, there was a greater proportion of younger people than would be usual. Some as young as seven or eight. Nathaniel didn't notice many over late twenties, although there were one or two. People stared as he walked by but not for long. They meandered along a concrete pathway until they got to a rectangular white building. Three stories high, lots of glass and a large double door entrance.

They went inside and Jimmy led Nathaniel to a large desk in the reception area.

'Hello, Debbie,' he greeted the young lady behind the desk.

'Jimmy,' she nodded.

'Looking for an import. Would have come in last night or yesterday late afternoon. Raggedy man here has allegedly lost his niece. Young, around …'

He turned to Nathaniel.

'Seven years old,' said the marine. 'Red-brown hair. Goes by Milly. Got a fur cape. Real smart.'

Debbie flicked through some cards. 'Here we go. Outside patrol found her wandering by herself. She got picked up by a bunch of Overlords. She escaped and ran for it. Claims her uncle was shot and killed.' Debbie looked at Nathaniel, raised an eyebrow.

The marine smiled. 'No, obviously not. They hit me on the head, knocked me down. She just got confused. When I came to, she was gone, so was my horse, my kit, my clothes and my axe. Had to dress myself in whatever rags I could find.'

Debbie glanced at the cards again. 'She's got your axe,' she said.

'What?'

'Your axe. When the patrol found her she was carrying a huge axe. Wouldn't put it down. The Chief Squire has it now. It's on the wall in his office.'

'Cool,' said Nathaniel as a wave of relief washed over him. 'If I could just pickup Milly and my axe then I'll be on my way. Thanks for all, I really appreciate it.'

Debbie shook her head. 'Sorry, raggedy man. That's not how things work here at the campus. We have rules. Structures and strictures. We'll need you to go downstairs to the holding rooms. Then I'll send a message up to the chief squire. We wait and see what he has to say then I, or someone else, will get hold of you in due time. Meanwhile, rest assured, Milly will be well taken care of. Jimmy, show raggedy man the way.'

The marine thought of cold cocking Jimmy, taking his rifle and demanding to see Milly but it was merely a fleeting though, replaced quickly by sanity and patience. After all, he reckoned to himself, a bit more thought before action and he might prevent a few more unnecessary deaths, all of them his own!

'Right, Jimmy,' he said. 'Show me the way.'

He followed the young man down a corridor and then down a flight of steps into the basement.

Jimmy unlocked the basement door and opened it. It was obvious that the basement had, at one stage, been used to store the files and supplies for the administration block. White concrete walls, unpainted floor, high barred windows that let in a pale, dust diminished light. Scattered around the room was a selection of sofas and wingback chairs. Some blankets and even a few pillows.

There were three people in the room, two men and a woman, standing and talking in hushed tones. They turned to stare at Nathaniel.

'See you later, raggedy man,' said Jimmy as he closed the door behind the marine.

The group stared at Nathaniel.

The marine stared back. Not aggressively, merely taking stock.

A lion, dressed in rags, locked in a basement in a university.

Eventually one of the men stepped forward and held out his hand.

'Hi. My name is Richmond. Richmond Baker. I am…well…I was a professor at this university. Comparative African Studies. You are?'

Nathaniel held out his hand and shook. The professor's hand was limp. Moist. Unpleasant.

'Master sergeant Nathaniel Hogan. United States Marine Corps.'

'You mean, ex-marine, don't you?'

Nathaniel shook his head. 'No, sir. Once a marine, always a marine.'

'Fine,' said Richmond. 'This here is Donald and Katie.'

The woman stepped forward and shook the marine's hand. Her grip was firm and dry. Her gaze direct. She was probably in her late forties. Flecks of gray in her hair. No makeup. Solid build but still very feminine. Nathaniel liked her immediately.

The third person, Donald, shuffled forward and held his left hand out. Nathaniel noticed that his right hand was curled into a ball and he held it in front of his chest.

The marine shook using his left hand. Donald mumbled something and then giggled. He held on to Nathaniel's hand for a while before Katie spoke.

'That's fine. Donald. You can let go now. Well done.'

Donald nodded and smiled. 'Donald do good,' he said. He ran his left hand through his hair a few times, pushing back hard. 'Donald does good.' Then he shuffled off and sat down on one of the sofas, hands between his knees. Smiling.

'Donald is special,' said Katie.

'Don't you mean, different,' countered Nathaniel.

'Technically it means the same thing. He is unusual. Uncommon. One of the patrols found him wondering around on the outside. He was brought in for processing.'

'Processing?' Questioned Nathaniel.

'Yes, you know. Tests. IQ, medicals, psychological.'

'Look, don't get me wrong,' said Nathaniel. 'But if high IQ and psych tests are the way to advancement here then Donald is in for a cold ride.'

Katie shook her head. 'Oh no, you see, Donald is a savant. An autistic savant. He can't drive or wire a plug, not that any of that matters any more, but watch this. Donald.'

Donald looked up at Katie.

'What is 377 multiplied by 795?'

'Two hundred and ninety nine thousand seven hundred and fifteen.'

Nathaniel shrugged. 'So. For all I know he's a hundred thousand out.'

Katie shook her head. 'We've been testing him all morning and then working the results out ourselves. He is always correct.'

'How does he do it?'

'He doesn't seem to actually calculate,' said Katie. 'From what I can gather, he sees numbers as colors and sounds and, somehow, blends them together to get the result.'

'Four hundred and seventy two,' said Donald.

'What's that, Donald?' Asked Katie.

Donald pointed at Katie's blouse. 'The number of stitches in your shirt. Four hundred and seventy two. Also, one thousand and nine.'

'What's that, sweetie?'

'Books. Books that I remember. I read one thousand and nine books and I remember them all.'

'You see,' said Katie to Nathaniel. 'He's literally a human long-term data storage facility. Regardless of IQ or other talents, the senior squire will find a use for him.'

'What about you and Richmond?'

'Well, Richy and I were upsetting the status quo.'

Richmond snorted. 'That's a polite way of saying that we pissed off the senior squire.'

'How?' Asked Nathaniel.

'We disagreed with him,' said Richmond. 'Told him that he was a goddamn Nazi and he and his elitist ideas should rot in hell.'

'Seems to me that he's not doing that bad of a job,' countered the marine.

'Nathaniel,' said Katie. 'Have you ever heard of eugenics?'

The marine shrugged. 'Sort of. Something about selective breeding? Preventing inbreeding. Promotion of superior traits.'

Katie nodded. 'Strictly speaking, that would be referred to as pseudo-eugenics. Pure eugenics goes many steps further. It goes beyond selective breeding to encompass actual extermination of people considered feeble minded, idle, insane, or simply unworthy.

The movement saw its zenith in the autumn of 1939 when Hitler approved the Aktion T-4 program. This authorized doctors and officials to carry out euthanasia of those the state deemed unworthy of life. Volunteer physicians coordinated the program from its headquarters in a villa in Berlin located at number 4 Tiergarten Street, hence the name T-4. Physicians at hospitals and psychiatric institutions throughout Germany identified and recommended candidates for euthanasia. At first, in accordance with the T-4 program, the physicians murdered 5000 congenitally deformed children.'

'5012,' interrupted Donald.

Katie smiled. 'Correct, Donald, 5012. Anyway, the children were starved to death at six special asylums that had been remodelled to accommodate the killings. Then, the T-4 program expanded to include adults, who were taken to killing asylums as well and starved. By August of 1941, almost 70,000 people had been killed under T-4.'

'Granted,' said Nathaniel. 'That was a terrible tragedy and one of the reasons that we fought a long and costly war against the Nazis. But I see no death camps or murder asylums here.'

Katie shook her head. 'Sergeant Hogan, what do you think would happen if a crippled child or so called "Feeble-Minded" person was denied any help and simply sent out into the world beyond this campus?'

Nathaniel didn't have to think. He had been out there for the last few months and he knew. 'They would die,' he said. 'They would starve to death within weeks.'

'So you see, sergeant,' said Katie. 'The senior squire does not need to build special asylums to starve the unworthy. The entire world has become his extermination camp. All that he has to do is turn them out and wait for them to die.'

'Bloody Nazi,' said Richmond with feeling.

Before any more could be said the door opened and two armed men strode in. 'Come on,' said the one. 'Professor Richmond, Doctor Katharine, Donald. It's time to see the senior squire.'

Once again Nathaniel contemplated simply taking the weapons of the two students and smacking them into unconsciousness but he decided against it. After all, no harm had come to him and the campus was a large place filled with a great many armed people.

The two men closed and locked the door after Richmond, Katie and Donald had left.

Nathaniel lay down on one of the sofas and closed his eyes.

An hour or so later, the door was opened and someone slid a tray in and then closed the door again. Nathaniel took a look. A bowl of stew, mainly tinned vegetables. A large jug of water. A plastic spoon. He ate and drank and then lay down again, sticking to the maxim of sleep when you can.

Through the small windows he could see the night approach. No one came with any more food but he still had sufficient water. There were no toilet facilities so he hoped that he wouldn't be held for too much longer. He decided that, come morning, he would give them a couple of hours and then simply smash the door down and make a plan from there.

The next morning, shortly after sunrise, the door opened and Jimmy walked in.

'Morning, raggedy man,' he greeted.

'Jimmy,' said Nathaniel.

'Come on. Follow me,' continued Jimmy. 'You got an appointment with the senior squire.'

Nathaniel followed the student up the stairs and out into the campus. Despite the early hour everybody seemed to be up and approaching the day with a purpose. Some carrying boxes of supplies, others dragging trolleys with water drums on, still others walking in groups with gardening utensils such as shovels and forks.

They continued walking until they came across a small man made lake. Situated on the one side, attached to a larger building, was a circular structure that looked a little like a bowl or teacup. Small base reaching up five stories to a flared out upper floor. Floor to ceiling windows looked out over the lake.

They went through the front entrance and the marine followed Jimmy up the stairs to the top floor. There were another two armed guards at the top of the stairwell. They greeted Jimmy and opened the doors for him. The double doors led into a reception area. A desk, some easy chairs. A young man sat behind the desk.

'Morning, Jimmy,' he greeted.

Jimmy nodded. 'Morning, Baxter. I brought the raggedy man to see the boss.'

'Thank you, Jimmy. Leave him and wait outside. We'll call when we need you.'

Jimmy gave a half salute and left.

Baxter took a card from a pile in front of him, clicked his ballpoint open and made a note on the top of the card. 'Please,' he said to Nathaniel. 'Sit down.'

Nathaniel sat down on a chair opposite Baxter's desk.

'So,' continued Baxter. 'Name?'

'Nathaniel Hogan. Master sergeant United States Marine Corps.'

Baxter wrote. 'Age?'

'Twenty eight.'

'Height and weight?'

'Six foot four or five, not sure. As for weight, well, who the hell weighs themselves in the current world order?'

Baxter glanced up. 'Let's say 230 pounds.'

'Whatever,' said Nathaniel. 'Say what you want.'

Baxter opened a drawer, pulled out a sheath of papers and slid them across the desk. Then he placed the pen on top.

'Mister Hogan, if you could just answer these simple questions. You have half an hour.' Baxter turned over a sand timer. 'Starting from now.'

Nathaniel shook his head. 'No. I don't think so.'

'Mister Hogan. Please don't make unnecessary waves. We have a system and it is working. Please, simply answer the questions and then we will reunite you with your niece and all will be as it should.'

Nathaniel pulled the pile of papers towards him and started reading

'Which word does not belong? Apple, marmalade, cherry, orange, grape.'

He sighed and began to write.

Before the sand had half drained he had finished and he passed the forms over to Baxter who started to mark them. After a few minutes he glanced up, a frown on his face.

'Have you taken this test before, mister Hogan?'

Nathaniel shook his head. 'No.'

'Wait here, please.' Baxter stood up, walked across the room and knocked on a door set in the sidewall of the office. Inside someone called for him to open.

He did so and walked in, closing the door behind him.

Nathaniel sat still and waited. Eventually Baxter came out.

'The senior squire will see you now,' he said as he held the door open.

Nathaniel stood up and walked over. As he entered the room he was hit by a little body running at full speed.

'Nate, you're safe.'

He picked Milly up and held her tight. 'Hello, sweetness,' he said. 'Are you alright?'

She nodded. 'The bad men took me after they shot you but I bit one and ran away. Then these people found me. They were very nice. They gave me food and porridge with as much sugar as I wanted.'

The marine put Milly down and looked across the room. Sitting behind a large desk was a pale-faced man. A shock of unruly dark hair, penetrating, pale blue eyes, thin long nose and heavy eyebrows. He was wearing a short sleeve shirt and his arms were painfully thin and so pale as to be almost iridescent, the blue of his veins showing clearly through the thin skin. But his force of character was a palpable thing. An aura of command. Power. Absolute belief.

Nathaniel ran his eyes over the rest of the room. A few filing cabinets. A table with a jug of water. Some pot plants. But the walls were covered with weapons. Ancient weapons. Pikes, swords, daggers, longbows, crossbows. And, hanging in pride of place behind the senior squire's desk, Nathaniel's axe.

He pointed at it. 'That's my axe.'

'Oh yes,' said the senior squire. Milly had it with her when we found her.'

Milly nodded. 'I grabbed it when I ran away. It's very heavy you know?'

'Yes,' said Nathaniel. 'I know. Well done, Milly.'

'It's a remarkable weapon, mister Hogan,' said the senior squire. 'Very unusual. Did you know that it harkens from the 8th century? Viking in construction. An extremely rare double head, unlike the usual Viking creations. Never before have I, or any of my colleagues, seen such a weapon in such a perfect condition. It is almost as though it has travelled through time to arrive here, unmarked and unsullied by age. Astonishing.'

'Yes,' said Nathaniel. 'Very. Now could I please have my axe back?'

The senior squire smiled. 'I think not, mister Hogan. Possession being nine tenths of the law and so on. I have a fascination for ancient weapons, mister Hogan, and that axe is one of my favourites.' The squire pointed at a seat in front of his desk. 'Take a seat, mister Hogan. Milly, you sit over there on the sofa.'

Nathaniel sat down, as did Milly.

'Have you ever taken an IQ test before, mister Hogan?' Asked the squire.

'Not to my knowledge.'

'I thought as much. Your results were very interesting. One might even say, alarming. You IQ shows up as a score of 152. You scored particularly highly on spatial awareness and visualization. Actually, you scored off the chart in both of those disciplines.'

The marine shrugged. 'So?'

'So, mister Hogan, it would appear that you are a certified genius. You register in the top one percentile of the world's most intelligent people. Albert Einstein had an IQ only a few points higher than yours, although, to be fair, it is substantially below mine.'

'Squire, this means nothing to me. I simply want my axe, my niece and to be left alone to go on my way.'

The squire pointed to one of the weapons hanging on the wall. 'Do you know what that is, mister Hogan?'

Nathaniel glanced over and nodded. 'English longbow. Six foot long, constructed from the heartwood of the Yew tree, capable of firing a three foot arrow under some one hundred and ten pounds of draw weight.'

The squire clapped. 'Delightful. You know your weapons, marine. Well done.'

He stood up, walked across the room and picked a different weapon off the wall. Then he sat down again. 'And what is this?' He asked Nathaniel.

'Medieval windlass crossbow. An inelegant weapon. Clumsy.'

The squire nodded. 'True. But, you see, mister Hogan. It is actually the more beautiful of the two weapons. The longbow is aesthetically pleasing. Deadly in the hands of a highly skilled operator. Someone who has literally been bred to the task over a lifetime of training. Someone much like you, master sergeant.

Whereas the crossbow…well, suffice to say that you can teach anyone to use a crossbow in a day. Three days tops. What elegance, what beauty in design. Such simplicity.'

The squire cranked the cross bow and slotted a bolt in.

'So, mister Hogan, I feel that you would be a very positive addition to our team. I would like to offer you a position. Sergeant at arms in charge of campus security. You see, mister Hogan, I have plans. This brave new world of ours is probably the best thing that could have happened to humanity. Every few millennia someone, or something, needs to press the reset button. Dinosaurs went their way and now the humanity of old must go theirs. We have a clean slate. With judicious selection and careful planning we can build a world that is populated by the worthy. The laudable. Achievers as opposed to spongers. Intellectual, noetic, rational people instead of uncultivated, lowbrow philistines.'

'Basically, stuff the stupid?'

The squire shook his head. 'No, that's not what I said. I said, to use the vernacular, stuff the unworthy.'

'And who decides who is unworthy?' Asked Nathaniel.

The squire raised an eyebrow. 'Why, the worthy, of course.'

'And who would decide who was worthy?'

The squire smiled, his eyes lit up and a glimmer of madness flickered through them. 'I would, mister Hogan. I would.'

'Thought so,' said Nathaniel. Then he turned to Milly.

'Milly, sweetheart, do me a favor. Go outside and tell Baxter that the squire and I are having a private chat.

Tell him that we are not to be disturbed. Then wait for me. Okay?'

Milly nodded. 'Okay.' She stood up off the sofa, walked to the door and left, closing it behind her.

'What was that about?' Asked the senior squire.

Hogan stood up. 'Where are Katie and Richmond?'

'Mister Hogan, that's none of your business.'

'I'm making it my business. Where are they?'

'They're safe.'

'Where?'

'Somewhere outside the perimeter. They were expelled late yesterday. They have been shunned.'

'Shunned?' Asked Nathaniel. 'You can't arbitrarily shun people because they disagree with you, you jerk off. Who do you think you are, the church of scientology, an Anabaptist priest? A bloody rabbi?'

The squire stood up and pointed the loaded crossbow at the marine. 'I am who I am, mister Hogan, and I recommend that you remember that.'

'You better put that thing down, boy,' growled Nathaniel. 'Before I take that bolt and ram it into your eye.'

The air around the marine shimmered slightly as the heat poured off him in waves, his adrenalin flow increasing at an exponential rate, his heart revving up to over three hundred beats a minute.

'And exactly how would you manage that, mister Hogan?'

'Easily, boy,' Hogan snapped his fingers. 'Like that. So put it down, give me my axe and then Milly and I will be on our way.'

The squire laughed. 'No. I think that we shall keep Milly. She passed all of the tests with flying colors. A very bright young girl. You, however, mister Hogan, I deem to be unworthy. Goodbye.'

The senior squire pulled the trigger. The arms of the crossbow sprang forward and launched the foot long steel bolt directly at Nathaniel's chest, traveling at around 190 feet per second.

But to Nathaniel's mega-enhanced senses it looked as though it was spiraling lazily through the air. A dragonfly. Or perhaps a bumblebee.

The marine sprang forward, plucked the bolt out of the air with his right hand, jumped the desk and landed in front of the squire. With his left hand he snatched the crossbow from his grasp, grabbed him by the neck and lifted him up against the wall.

'Squire,' he said. 'You have been deemed unworthy.'

And he slammed the steel bolt into the squire's right eye.

The strike was so powerful that the bolt penetrated the skull and drove itself two inches into the masonry behind it. Nathaniel turned, walked across the room and took his axe down. Behind him the body of the squire hung on the wall like some obscene work of art.

Then marine opened the door, exited and closed it behind him.

'Baxter,' he said to the receptionist. 'The senior squire is not to be disturbed under any circumstances. He has a lot on his mind right now and needs to think.'

He picked Milly up and put her on his shoulders. 'Come on, Milly. Let's be on our way.'

They left the campus via the main gates, picked up Nathaniel's shotgun and ammo from the hedge and headed north once more.

Chapter 14

Jarvis Baker sniffed and wiped his nose with the back of his hand. He had just finished his breakfast, a bowl of acorn gruel with dried fish.

He stood up and donned his stiff leather jerkin and pulled on his new riding boots, both of these items were goblin-made and courtesy of the Fair-Folk. He and three of his friends had been issued them when they had joined up with the Cornwall First Horse Regiment the week before. He tied his yellow silk scarf around his neck to complete the uniform. Red scarves donated private. Yellow were corporals and blue were sergeants. He glanced at himself in the mirror and smiled.

He was a cavalryman. And an officer. Jarvis had never excelled at school either in the classroom or on the sports field, but he had always been an adequate horse rider. Now he was in a position of power. A position of responsibility. Whilst people like Jake Pardon who had been the school rugby captain, and Mildred Stannard who had been the brightest in the school, were both fishermen and fish gutters. There would be no cushy city job for Mildred, no professional sports job for Jake.

But for Jarvis, the world was his oyster and he had already begun to dine on its heady delights.

Jarvis's father came stomping down the stairs into the living room. He looked at the nineteen-year-old boy and sneered.

'Off to play soldiers, boy?'

Jarvis ignored him.

'Talking to you, boy.'

'No you're not, father,' said Jarvis. 'You're just causing trouble. Leave it out, okay?'

'Those things. Those pig-men and their hoity-toity masters, them ain't your friends, boy. Trust me on this.'

'Dad, we were starving before they came. Gangs of vagrants were roaming the land. Society was breaking down. Now we are safe. We eat. We live.'

'Aye,' nodded Jarvis's father. 'We live. As long as we behave, we live. They're asking for female volunteers now. To clean and sew and cook for them. Servants. Servants to the hoity-toities and their pig-men.'

'I know,' said Jarvis. 'I've told Doris to try out.'

Jarvis's father slammed his fist down on the dining table. 'No!' He shouted. 'No daughter of mine will be seen dead in that camp. Who knows what could happen. Pig-men and goblins and monsters. And the pretty masters. I don't trust them.'

'She's sixteen, father. She can do what she wants.'

'No. My house, my rules. I can't stop you becoming a lackey to them but I can stop Doris and I will.'

Jarvis opened the front door. 'You are pathetic, father. Pathetic.'

The young man slammed the door behind him.

The father stood still for a while and then his face crumpled in anguish. 'Yes, my boy,' he whispered. 'I am pathetic. But I'm right. There is something wrong here, I just don't know what it is.'

Outside Jarvis greeted two of his friends who had joined him for the walk to the stables. Benny and Gavin were similar to Jarvis. Less than adequate students and general all round non-achievers. Not layabouts, as such, merely incompetent. Loners through their inability to attract friends as opposed to by choice.

But now they all had friends. They were part of the elite. The Cornwall first horse. Brothers in arms. They walked through the Orc built stockade and to the stables. Waiting for them was Sergeant Snark, a goblin who was nominally in charge of the first horse, even though he himself could not go near any of the horses without risk of serious injury. He was more a planner and a quartermaster than a field commander. But, as the first horse was not, strictly speaking, a combat regiment, that didn't matter. As long as they listened to orders and had all of the equipment that they needed, then everything was good. They delivered messages, scouted out the land and carried urgent supplies.

There were just over sixty of them already and every day more volunteered for service. They stood in military rows outside the stables and waited for Snark to address them. He climbed onto a wooden platform so that all could see him. In his right hand he held a sword. Almost three foot long with a large guard. Its broad blade was slightly curved and it looked clumsy and ill balanced. A blade for hacking and hewing as opposed to delicate swordsmanship. In his other hand he held a lance. Basically a six foot long stick with a steel point attached to the end.

'Cavaliers,' he said. 'Commander Ammon has deemed it necessary for you to carry weapons. Every man shall be issued with a sword and a lance. This is a great honor and shows our commander's depth of trust and love for the humans. Long may he live.' Sergeant Snark held the lance high and shouted the Fair-Folk battle cry 'Kamateh!'

The humans joined in.

'Kamateh! Kamateh!'

More goblins came from around the back of the stables carrying swords and lances that they issued to the cheering humans.

Jarvis accepted his sword and lance with a salute. But, as he strapped the blade on, he felt ill at ease. Because he knew that these weapons had not been given to them in order to be used on Orcs or goblins. No, these weapons were for raiders. Or dissenters. Or for whomever the commander said they were for.

They were perfect killing tools. Perfect, that is, for killing humans.

He decided that, when he got home, he would tell Doris to think for a while before volunteering to serve the Fair-Folk.

Just for a while.

Simply to be safe.

Chapter 15

'You stop right there, boy,' said the old lady. Her shotgun pointing unwaveringly at Nathaniel's chest. 'Heard you coming from a mile off. You walks like some sort of hephalump or sumting.'

The marine smiled and put down the sack that he was carrying over his shoulder. 'I be's quite ef me wah be, gramma. I was warning yuh wid me noises. I means nuh harm and I come inna peace.'

The old lady burst out laughing. 'Yuh are a naughty mon,' she said. 'And yuh speak di patois.'

'My name is Nathaniel Hogan. Master sergeant, United Sates Marine Corps. This here is my niece, Milly.'

The old lady stared at the two of them for a while and then lowered the shotgun. 'She ain't your neice, dat for sure. But she look happy and well cared for, so dat good enough fo me.' She turned and called out. 'Adalyn, Janeka. Come outta da bushes and greets this nice mon.'

Two teenage girls emerged from the hedgerow. They were late teens, similar enough to be sisters. Long braided hair, tall. Slim but still buxom enough for their figures to be apparent through the bulky jackets they were wearing. Both carried shotguns. Single barrel twelve bores.

They approached the marine and held their hands out.

'Adalyn,' said the slightly taller one.

Nathaniel shook her hand. Her grip was strong, firm and dry.

The other girl proffered her hand.

'Janeka,' she said. Her grip was softer and she held on for a heartbeat longer than Adalyn. Her gaze was more direct and her lips tilted in a slight smile that seemed to be a permanent feature.

Then the two of them introduced themselves to Milly who immediately started to tell them a long rambling story about where they had been and what had happened. The story jumped around so outrageously that it was impossible to follow. But the girls listened anyway and ooh'ed and ah'ed when they felt it to be appropriate.

Meanwhile, the old lady took Nathaniel aside and, it was only when the marine stood close to her that he noticed her size. She was at least six foot tall and broad to go with it. Her features, although old, were still fine and her laugh lines showed a character capable of warmth and humor.

'My name be Gramma Higgins.' She put her hand out to shake. It felt like a rubber glove filled with sticks and pebbles. Strong and callused. 'These girlies be my nieces.'

'Pleased to make your acquaintance, Gramma. So where are you girls from?'

'Just outside Birmingham. Our boys, dat be me nephews, three of them, they be in Afghanistan. Me daughter, she be in London looking for work when they electrics go out. The girls' father, him be a useless son of a bitch and he long gone. There be no food where we was so we took to the countryside. Bin survivin' on bugs and crickets and birdies and the like. If I eat another burdock root I'm gonna be sick. You know, before this I was a fine figure of a woman. Now I just all faded away and crinkle-skin from lack of food.

Mind you, those two girlies done lost a couple hundred pounds between them and they look, ooee, so fine.'

Nathaniel glanced over at the two girls and Gramma Higgins was right. They did look, ooee, so fine indeed.

The marine laughed. 'Where you camping, Gramma?' He asked.

'We's back in the bushes there,' Gramma pointed. 'Come, I shows you.'

Nathaniel picked up his sack of goods and the four of them followed Gramma back into the shrubs.

Nathaniel was impressed. The camp was secluded; a light screen of branches laced between trees ensured that, unless you actually walked into it, it was out of line of sight. There was a small depression in which the remains of a fire smoldered softly. And perhaps twenty meters away, there was a fast flowing stream that ran with enough volume to avoid icing up.

The marine asked the girls to fetch more firewood while he built up the fire with what was available. Then he took the two rabbits that he had trapped the night before from his sack and skinned and jointed them. He threw the meat into a pot with some water and left it to simmer while he went for a walk to look for more ingredients. At the same time he set four rabbit snares along the trail.

It didn't take him long to find a ring of large mushrooms. He picked them and then went down to the steam to pick some bulrushes. He cut out the white stem of the bullrushes and then went back to the camp where he diced the mushrooms and bullrush stems and put them into the pot. Finally he harvested a large handful of nettles and those went into the pot to provide a spicy, peppery taste.

He let the stew cook for an hour and then served it up.

At the end of the meal Gramma Higgins burped long and loud and then laughed. 'Better out than in, I always says,' she said. 'Now, Nathaniel, dat was the bestest meal I have had for a long time. You is one serious genius at finding foods in the outdoors.'

The other girls agreed.

After the pot had been cleaned they sat around the fire a chatted. Actually, they sat around the fire and listened to Gramma talk.

She told Nathaniel about their journey and how they had stayed alive thus far. It seemed that their continued existence had been brought about mainly by hiding. Staying out of harms way and scrounging a living off the land.

She finished by asking the marine where he was heading.

'North.'

'Dats it? Just, north. No specific place?'

Nathaniel thought for a moment. 'Far north. Scotland.'

'Why?'

'Many reasons. Firstly, I reckon if I find a place that's so rural and backwoods then it won't have been affected by the pulse. Secondly, well, I've sort of been told to go there.'

'By who?'

Nathaniel laughed. 'You wouldn't believe me if I told you.'

'Try me,' said Gramma.

'An old, blind, traveler lady and some druids at Stonehenge,' he held up his hand to show Gramma the scar.

'They gave me this.'

Gramma stared at the symbol. 'So when were you at Stonehenge?'

The marine shook his head. 'Never been there. It happened in a dream.'

'You got a scar from a dream?'

'Yep. Told you that you wouldn't believe me.'

'What's not to believe, my boy,' disagreed Gramma. 'I believes. Why would you lie? I just wonders what's in store for you when you gets north.'

Nathaniel grinned. 'Me too, Gramma. Me too.'

Gramma stood up, her knees popping as she did. 'Well, girls,' she said. 'It sleepy time. Come on, Milly, you too.'

Milly kissed Nathaniel goodnight and followed Gramma and the other two girls to their shelter.

The marine sat next to the fire, staring at the flames. Then, as was his habit, he concentrated and tried again to conjure up the ball of flame that the old gypsy had shown him. But, once again, he was unsuccessful. However, he kept at it.

'Dat's not how you do it.'

Nathaniel started in shock. Gramma Higgins had snuck up so quietly that he hadn't heard her.'

Hey, Gramma,' he said. 'You move awful quite for an old bird.'

Gramma chuckled. 'Me old but me not cold. At least not yet.' She sat down opposite Nathaniel. 'I see'd the Obeah man, voodoo priest, do that once.'

'What?'

'You trying to make light. Or maybe fire, I's not sure. I's gifted but only wid da sight, me I can't conjour worth crap. Only I can see. And I see's that you ain't doing it right.'

'What am I doing wrong then?' Asked Nathaniel 'I'm concentrating as hard as I can. I believe. What's my problem?'

'Your problem, my boy,' said Gramma. 'Is dat you concentrating too much. Much too much. First you'se gots to clear your mind. Relax. Then dissipate. Let you spirit flow from you body and meld wid da trees and da earth and da sky. Be all. Be everyting. Do it now.'

Nathaniel sat still and let his mind flow. He could feel the whispering of the trees, he felt their ponderous heart beat as they drew sap through their veins. He felt the awesome solidity of the earth; he felt its age and its life giving properties. He soared into the sky and listened to the winds exaltation as it flew across the heavens. He was nowhere. He was everywhere.

'Now,' said Gramma. 'take a little bit of energy from all that you feel. A little wind, a tiny portion of sap, a pinch of the Earth's great power. Reel it in like a fisherman pulling in a net. Bring it close. Closer and closer. Can you see it?'

Nathaniel nodded.

'Good,' continued Gramma. 'Now bring it to you right hand. Pull it in. Hold it in the palm of your hand. You see it there?'

Again Nathaniel nodded.

'Right,' continued Gramma. 'Now tell it what you want it to be.'

And out of nothing came light. And heat. And, suspended above Nathaniel's right hand was as small ball of flame. Shimmering and coruscating. Spinning slowly as it crackled and hummed. The marine closed his hand around it and it winked out of existence.

He smiled at Gramma.

'Thank you, Gramma Higgins.'

The old lady waved his thanks away. 'Was nothing. You's got da gift, my boy. You got it most powerful dat I ever did see. You be careful with it. Fire burns. Fire gets outta control. And fire can destroy as easy as it can warm. Next time you do it, try something else. Maybe ice.'

The old lady rose once again and headed back to her shelter.

Nathaniel curled up next to the fire and slept.

***

The next morning Nathaniel rose before sunrise and spent an hour tapping Birch trees for their sap. Then he collected a sack of Burdock roots and walked back to camp.

For breakfast he made his Burdock root and sap porridge. The meal was hot and nourishing and sweet. Gramma Higgins was amazed.

'Boy,' she said to the marine. 'You'se one star in the cooking area. If I but be fifty years younger I be testing to see you as good in the bedding department.'

Adalyn and Janeka both giggled loudly. Milly looked puzzled.

Nathaniel laughed. 'I be jus fine in that department, Gramma,' he said. 'Just fine.'

'Well,' Gramma continued with a twinkle in her eyes. 'You'se is mighty tall. I jus hope dat all be in proportion.'

'Gramma,' observed the marine.' If everything was in proportion den I be over seven feet tall.'

Gramma slapped her thighs and laughed until she started to choke.

Adalyn patted her on the back until the fit stopped and Gramma shrugged her off.

'Quit be beating your Gramma, Adalyn. Not needs to keep a-thumpin me like that.'

'Sorry, Gramma,' said Adalyn with a grin. 'My mistake.'

Gramma stroked Adalyn's hair. 'You'se a good girl. Now clean up de dishes and pots, quick now.'

Within an hour Nathaniel had harvested his rabbit traps and collected four fat rabbits. He gutted and skinned them while the girls decamped and, although no one had mentioned it, it seemed natural that they were a group and would stick together. They walked slowly and easily all day heading north, stopping once, briefly, for a light lunch of boiled sap.

That night they set camp and the marine cooked a rabbit stew. They chatted around the fire. Light conversation, laughs and giggles from the girls. Milly smiled a lot. An oasis of happiness in a world of darkness.

Then they went to bed and the marine practiced his enchantments, calling up the ball of fire with ease. Suddenly, in a fit of childish mischief, he sent the ball rocketing into the heavens like a 4th of July rocket.

Afterwards, satisfied, he curled up and went to sleep.

***

'It was from over there,' said the tall man, pointing in the direction of Nathaniel's camp. 'Looked like a flare. Or a rocket, shooting up into the sky. Means that there has got to be something of note where it came from. And it's close now. I can smell the fire.'

'I can smell food,' said one of the other men.

The third man merely sniffed the air and nodded in general agreement.

The tall man dismounted and tied his horse's reins to a low branch.

'Come on,' he said. 'We go on foot from here on. Quieter that way.'

The other two climbed off their horses and hitched them, to the same branch. The shorter men drew long cavalry swords from their saddlebags. The tall man carried a bolt action .22 rifle. All of them wore long, black fur coats, obviously taken from a de rigueur outfitter in one of the Home Counties. Underneath, stout woolen shirts, jeans and top-of-the-line hiking boots.

They ghosted through the dark towards the camp, rolling their feet slowly so as to avoid crunching the snow. Picking each footstep with care. Their carriage and demeanor spoke of military training. And their appearance did not lie. All three had been dishonorably discharged from the Queens Suffolk Guards for stealing weapons and trading them for drugs. After spending four years in military confinement they were sent on their way. They had stayed together ever since, for some two years now, surviving on state handouts and petty theft.

The pulse and the following breakdown of society was the best thing that had ever happened to them.

The tall one raised a clenched fist, pointed at one of the others and then pointed towards his own eyes. The man nodded and moved forward while the other two men waited.

Five minutes later he came back. They put their heads close together.

'One bivouac,' the reconnaissance man whispered. 'Three, maybe four women inside. No men. It's a bloody take away.'

The tall man sniggered. 'Well then, let's go and help ourselves.' He stood upright and started walking. Their need for silence no longer needed. For they were kings of the night. They were the evil that men do.

And then – the real night came alive. A shadow boiled up from the ground and became solid. A Man, dressed in rags. A double headed war axe. The sound of metal striking flesh.

The reconnaissance man grunted and fell forward. As he hit the ground his body lay still but his head kept going. Rolling like some obscene bowling ball.

The shadow man moved, disappeared. Reappeared. The battle axe swung again; rising up from low it struck the second man under his chin and cleft his face in twain. Brains and gore and blood fountained skyward.

The tall man raised the rifle. But there was a blinding flash of pain and, when he looked down, the rifle was lying on the snow. As were both of his hands. He threw back his head to unleash a howl of agony but the axeman stepped forward and covered his mouth, stifling all sound.

Then the raggedy man shook his head. 'No noise,' he said. 'It would be impolite to wake up the girls. They need their beauty sleep.'

The tall man felt the axe against his leg, close to his groin. There was a feeling of pressure. Then more pain flowed through him. He realized that the axeman had cut his femoral artery.

And his last living sight was that of two deep green eyes staring at him with utter contempt.

The marine let the body drop to the ground and then set about stripping them of anything useful. Their fur coats, weapons, the taller man's boots that happened to be a size 13, perfect for Nathaniel, and his woolen shirt. Even the tall man's blood soaked jeans.

He tied everything in a bundle using one of the coats and set off to fetch the horses.

He tied the horses up next to a low branch near the camp then he went down to the stream. He sat down next to the fast flowing water and conjured up a ball of light. Then he moved the ball, through the air, so that it hovered in front of him. Satisfied, he started to rinse the blood from the clothes using the clean running water.

Afterwards, he extinguished the light and walked back to the camp where he built up the fire and hung the wet clothes over branches near the flames so that they could dry.

He lay down once again and went to sleep, reminding himself to wake up in a couple of hours.

The marine was up just before the sun. The furs and jeans were dry and the cold water had gotten rid of the blood. Firstly, Nathaniel used twine to clumsily stitch the rent in the jeans, then he stripped the rags off his legs and slid the jeans on. They felt stiff and the stitching itched slightly but, compared to his previous rags, they were fantastic. Next, he cut the coats up and, once again, constructed himself a long flowing fur coat and a two blankets.

Then he pulled the rags off his torso, donned the clean wool shirt and tied the cloak on.

The pleasure of his new clothes made him grin and he stroked the fur, marveling at its warmth and softness.

'From rags to riches,' he mumbled to himself.

'Talkin' to yourself, boy?' Asked Gramma, who had, once again, snuck up on the marine without him hearing her.

'Jesus, Gramma,' exclaimed Nathaniel. 'How you gets to move so quiet?'

'Well, you knows what they say, the older the moon the brighter it shines. I see dat you got yourself some new items of clothing. Pray tell, boy, where dey come from?'

'Some men, last night. Wanted to do bad things. I stopped them. They didn't need their clothes anymore.'

'How many?'

'Three. Look,' Nathaniel pointed at the horses that were tethered behind to a bush. 'Horses. Also got a couple of nice swords for Adalyn and Janeka and a little .22 rifle for Milly.'

Gramma stared at the marine for a while, then she spoke. 'You kill three men last night and I don't hear but a whisper?'

Nathaniel nodded.

'You good at what you do, boy,' said Gramma.

The marine said nothing as he walked to the horses to fetch the weapons.

'And de raggedy man stepped forth from de shadows,' whispered Gramma. 'And, lo, the light showed him in his true form. And the people were afraid, for the raggedy man was Death himself and he came for all.'

She crossed herself and shivered with superstitious awe.

Chapter 16

Commander Ammon was less than happy. He hadn't seen this coming and, quite frankly, he wasn't sure what to do about it.

'Orc sergeant Teg came to me last week,' said Seth. 'He reported that large amounts of weapons were no longer to be found in the stores. We searched everywhere but they could not be found. So, I cast a minor seek and find enchantment on the stores. We were able to track down the latest batch of missing goods. It appears that a human from the village of Pennance has been taking them.'

Ammon thought for a while. Theft was a concept that the Fair-Folk were not familiar with. They themselves wanted for nothing, the Orcs and goblins were bred for battle and carrying out certain tasks, theft not being one of them, and the constructs did not think at all unless instructed to.

'What does the human do with them?'

'It seems to be storing them. Some 50 crossbows, 400 bolts, ten swords and shields.'

'What for?'

'I have a theory,' said Seth.

'Go ahead.'

'The word, sedition, comes to mind.'

Ammon shook his head. 'I do not understand. What do the humans have to rebel about?'

Seth was as baffled as the commander, but he had given it some thought.

'They are an independent species,' he said. 'Many of them seem to value their freedom above all else. They see us as their leaders and this causes umbrage.'

'But we are their leaders,' argued Ammon. 'Have we not organized a system of trade, have we not stopped the wholesale banditry, have we not provided food? We lead. They must follow. It is for their own good.'

'I agree.'

'So,' said Ammon, 'What do you suggest?'

'Harsh discipline. As a race they understand violence. We need to show that we are hard but fair masters.'

'Corporal punishment?' Suggested Ammon. 'Perhaps sixty lashes?'

Seth shook his head. 'Capital punishment. I suggest that we show him the gallows as soon as possible. We need to stop this before it spreads. As we have seen before, they can be a tenacious and stubborn race and we need to stamp out any possible thoughts of sedition.'

'Make it so,' said the commander. 'Who is it?'

'A male human called Robert Baker. I shall send a message to Orc sergeant Gog who is in charge of the Pennance battalion. He shall see the punishment carried out by tomorrow morning at first light.'

***

Benny rushed into Jarvis's room, banging the door open. Breathless.

'Whoa, partner,' said Jarvis. 'What gives with the huge rush?'

Benny stood for a while, catching his breath.

'It's about your uncle Robert. Gerry just arrived with a message. He wasn't meant to read it but, well you know, we all do.'

'So?' Urged Jarvis.

'Uncle Robert has been charged with sedition. Stealing weapons from the Fair-Folk. They're readying the gallows. Jarvis, they're going to hang Robert at sunrise.'

'They can't do that.'

'They can. And they will. There's no way that we can stop them.'

Jarvis stood up and strapped on his sword.

'What you doing?' Asked Benny.

'I'm going to speak to father. He was right. Now, somehow, we need to save uncle Robert and then get the hell out of here.'

The two friends ran down the main street towards the bay where they found Jarvis's father, mending his fishing nest.

Jarvis blurted out the story and waited for his father's reaction.

He threw his net down and snorted in disgust. 'Shit. That bloody younger brother of mine. Always knew he would end up over his head. Dammit. Come on, boys.'

Jacob Baker started walking back home and the two young men followed.

'What are we going to do, pa?' Asked Jarvis as they got home.

Jacob didn't answer. He simply went to the hallway cupboard and pulled out two double-barreled shotguns. He loaded them with buckshot and then opened a drawer in the cupboard. Inside the drawer was a glass jar filled with copper pennies. He poured a handful of pennies into each shotgun barrel and then, tearing four strips of a shoe polish rag, he pushed wadding down each barrel to prevent the coins falling out.

Then he smiled. But it was a mere grim facsimile of humor. A death's head grin as opposed to an expression of happiness.

'Ha,' he said. 'Let's see those bastard pig-men try to stand up against a barrel load of his majesties coin of the realm. So, when do they reckon that they're going to string up my little brother?'

'Sunrise tomorrow, mister Baker,' answered Benny.

'Right. Jarvis, I want you to go and find your sister, Doris. I'm going to take one of the horses, you take the other three. Pack everything that you can. Food, medical supplies, knives, the pistol next to my bed. Make sure you take an extra pair of boots. Then the both of you head north, away from these Fair-Folk bastards. This village is not going to be healthy for any of the Baker family after tomorrow.'

'But, dad,' argued Jarvis. 'How am I going to help you rescue uncle Robert?'

Jacob smiled again. This time it was genuine. 'Son, how many pig-men and goblins are stationed here?'

Jarvis shrugged. 'Not sure, dad. A thousand. Maybe two thousand.'

'And how many will be watching the murder of my brother?'

'All of them, I suppose.'

'Exactly. Look, son, ever since your mother passed we haven't got on so well. But I tried my best. I did what I thought was right.'

'And you were right, dad. I know that now. So, let's save uncle Robert and then get out of here.'

Jacob put his arm around his son. 'My boy, I'm sorry. But I'm not going to save Robert, there's simply no way that we could. I'm going to die with him. And at least make a few of these pig-men pay for the privilege of murdering my baby brother. Jarvis, my time here has passed. I no longer care or even have the will to continue. Every day I ache for your mother's company. I love you and Doris with all my heart but you have to let me go. It's all that I ask to go out in a blaze of glory.' Jacob laughed. 'It'll be fun. Also, it will give you a head start.'

Silent tears ran down Jarvis's face.

The father and son hugged one last time and then Jacob left, concealing his shotguns under his long, fishermen's coat.

Jarvis and Doris left Pennance later that evening, slipping out under the cover of darkness. But they did not go alone. With them was Gerry, his brother, and his parents. Each had their own horse.

They headed north.

***

Jacob sat atop his horse that stood on the small hill overlooking the Orc encampment. He was watching his final sunrise. And, as if it knew, and did not want to disappoint, it breached the horizon in a burst of deep lavender. Then the streaks of purple turned slowly to pink and then gold as the massive orb floated upwards. The eternal aurora borealis lights flickered their green wash across the heavens in a perfect counterpoint. A new day had been birthed.

Below him the entire Pennance battle battalion was arrayed outside of the stockade. Massed ranks of alien creatures.

Alongside them stood a group of the village noteworthies, perhaps twenty or so. Councilman

Blamey, father Donovan and doctor Brennan amongst them.

In the small clearing in front of the crowd stood a plain wooden gallows. There was no trapdoor or hanging drop as the structure had been built at ground level. It was a simple L shape from which a rope hung. The rope would be placed around Robert's neck and he would be hauled up and held until he choked to death.

A goblin started a slow beat on a skin drum and the compound gates opened to reveal the prisoner, flanked by two Orcs. They walked slowly through the massed ranks until they reached the gallows.

Jacob leant forward and patted his mare on the neck.

'Come on, girl,' he whispered. 'Let' go make some noise.'

He kicked her flanks and she leapt into a gallop.

The ranks of Orcs and goblins glanced up at the sound of the thundering hooves to see a single man bearing down on them. His head was thrown back and he was whooping a battle cry.

Robert saw him coming and he shouted back. An incoherent cry of both pride and disbelief.

Jacob spurred his horse across the front of the crowd, urging every bit of speed out of it. But before he got half way there, the goblin archers had started to unleash their arrows.

Jacob flicked back his long coat and drew one of his shotguns. He aimed and fired back at the goblins, discharging both barrels at once. The combination of buckshot and copper pennies swathed through them, like a claymore mine, tearing off limbs and hammering half-inch holes through their alien torsos.

A group of Orcs jumped in front of the fisherman. He dropped his empty shotgun, drew the next and fired. Again the discharge wreaked havoc and devastation.

An arrow struck the horse in the neck and it went down. Jacob sprang from its back as it did and ran the last few feet to his brother. He pulled his knife out and slashed the ropes from his hands.

The sun grew dark as over five hundred goblin archers unleashed their cloth yard arrows at once. The air was filled with the sound of fluting death as the arrows reached their zenith and plunged down towards the two brothers.

They put their arms around each other and smiled.

***

Later that day, when the orcs went to collect the stolen arms from Roberts's barn they were no longer there. Instead there was but a simple note written on a scrap of brown paper.

"There will be blood for blood!"

Chapter 17

His full name was Cornelius Montgomery Thaddeus Parkinson. It was a long name. His friends, when they had still been alive, had called him Tad. Some said because it was a shortening of Thaddeus. Others because it was short for Tadpole.

It wasn't easy living up to such a long name. Especially when you had Achondroplasia or, as many referred to it as, dwarfism. Tad stood four foot five and weighed in at 140 pounds. And that was all muscle and bone.

Thaddeus had been born to a mother, who was a full time housewife and a father who was a teacher at the local elementary school. They had been good and kind parents and Tad's affliction was never treated as such. Both parents gave him full rein to whatever he wanted to do and supported him fully. He qualified from Edinburgh University, at the age of 25, with an honors degree in astronomy.

By this stage he had also become a minor celebrity as Britain's only dwarfish bodybuilder. Ever wary of obesity problems that many achnondroplasts suffered from, Tad had become a fanatical exerciser and weight lifter. The bodybuilding side of it was merely a byproduct of his four-hour a day training regime.

It was after he had graduated that he had his first real argument with his parents. At the age of twenty-five with a respected degree behind his name, Cornelius Montgomery Thaddeus Parkinson (Tad), decided to join Burnaby's traveling circus as a strongman act.

Tad certainly knew that he was being deliberately obtuse and otherwise. But he had his reasons and they were his own. At the same time that he joined Burnaby's he took up knife throwing. As with everything that he did he became superb. Probably the best in the United Kingdom, if not the world.

Sometimes people still made jokes about dwarf throwing or they asked him where his axe was or they called him Gimli. But they seldom did it more than once. And that wasn't because he always resorted to violence. In fact he often turned the clumsy humor back on people gaining both their respect and their friendship.

For the last three weeks, however, he had taken to talking to himself. This was because, out of the forty people that had worked in the traveling circus, he was the only one still living. And he was lonely.

The pulse had hit while they were on the road and, after it had become obvious that the cars and trucks were not going to miraculously all start to work again, they had pushed them off the road into an adjacent field, forming them into a round laager or encampment.

A stream ran across the bottom of the clearing and, amongst them all, they had sufficient food for about a week.

Unfortunately, mister Burnaby was a class 1 diabetic and his insulin ran out at about the same time as the food. He went into a diabetic coma that evening and never came around.

From then on the lifestyle at the lager became a comedy of errors. Whilst grieving her husband's death, Mrs. Burnaby had a heart attack and died. Faced with a double funeral, they decided to dig a single large grave fairly far away from the encampment. Zorba, the male half of the Flying Greek Trapeze Artists, slipped while digging the grave and cut his leg quite badly. Without antibiotics the wound became infected and turned gangrenous within hours.

Later sepsis set in and Zorba died an agonizing death in the small hours of that morning. Adelpha couldn't take the death of her beloved husband and slashed her wrists necessitating another double funeral.

They dug the second grave next to the first.

Then Dorcas Pugsley, the bearded fat lady, collected a basket of mushrooms and made a mushroom stew for all. Fortunately she guzzled most of it down herself leaving only enough for six of the road crew to snack on.

By midday next all seven had died in the throes of unimaginable pain.

It took two days to dig a big enough grave for all of them.

At the end of the second week one of the five clowns found an ancient unopened can of pickled fish under the floorboards of their caravan and the resultant battle for it caused the immediate death of three of them. The two victors shared the fish.

Within twelve hours they started to suffer from blurred vision, dry mouth and muscle weakness. 72 hours later they had died of botulism poisoning.

No one bothered to bury them. They simply dragged them off into the forest and left them there.

Tad went hunting for small game and, using his prodigious knife throwing abilities, he managed to kill a couple of pigeons. However, to his shame, he told no one and simply cooked and ate them himself before he returned to the camp. He kept up this subterfuge for another ten days, by which time the remaining 23 members of the circus were almost dead from starvation. Tad knew that, even if he hunted all day, he could never find enough food for all, so he simply kept his deeds secret. But the rest were now aware that, somehow, Tad was getting food.

That evening when Tad reappeared from his days hunting they attacked him en masse, determined to find out where his food supply was. It was a pathetic and unbelievably depressing show of strength as the score of emaciated, starving, sickly people attempted to physically best the well-fed, healthy circus strongman.

More than half of them died from straightforward exertion as their floundering hearts simply gave up beating due to lack of sustenance. With deep sadness and massive remorse, Tad had to kill the rest in order to live on.

And so he had. The only survivor of the world's blackest farce.

Since then he had taken to talking to himself, hanging tenuously onto his last threads of sanity in a world gone absolutely and completely mad.

He glanced up at the horizon and saw a small group of three horses and riders silhouetted against the lowering sun. He quickly donned his leather jerkin, a custom made waistcoat with enough small pockets to hold a dozen razor sharp throwing knives. Then he slipped on his leg sheaths, one on each thigh. Each of these held a single larger, heavyweight-throwing knife. Finally, he slid one of his steel tomahawks into a loop on his belt. Then he climbed up onto the roof of one of the trucks that made up the laager and he waited.

The group ambled up towards him and stopped a few feet away.

A large man with a small girl riding in front of him raised his hand in greeting.

'Nathaniel Hogan,' he said. 'Master sergeant, United States Marine Corps. This is Milly, these two lovelies are Adalyn and Janeka and this be Gramma Higgins.'

Tad nodded his acknowledgement. 'I be Tad, astrologer, circus strongman, knife thrower, survivor and dwarf. I have no one to introduce on account of all of them being dead. I think that I may be insane…but that remains to be proven in any sort of empirical way. At present it is simply a working theory. Welcome to my laager.'

The party dismounted and led their horses in between two trucks and into the protection of the laager.

'So, how long have you been here, Tad?' Asked Nathaniel.

'A while. Since the solar storm. There were many more of us. It's a long story and I have no desire to speak of it. At times I am no longer even sure if it all happened. In fact, I am no longer sure if this is all real or simply some manner of delusion. Regardless,' he continued. 'It is the structure in which I am being forced to operate so, until further proof, I shall continue to assume that it is a reality of some sort.'

The marine smiled. 'Tad, you are one weird dude.'

Tad nodded. 'Perhaps. Perhaps not. Who knows.'

'Do you have any food?' Enquired Nathaniel.

'No. But I can get food. I hunt well.'

'Well, then,' said the marine. 'Why don't we let the ladies start up a good fire while you and I go and hunt us up a mess of something.'

Tad nodded. 'Let's go. Better done than said.' He climbed down from the truck roof and he and Nathaniel headed away from the laager and towards the nearby forest.

They walked without talking for a while. Nathaniel was impressed at the way that Tad moved. His footsteps made no sound, he kept to the shadows and his gaze constantly swept the surrounds.

Then Tad held his hand up and put a finger to his lips. He pointed.

Nathaniel stared for a few seconds before his eyes translated the scene in front of him. And when it did, it was immediately apparent.

Standing in the dappled shade, cropping the grass, was a small Muntjac deer, maybe forty feet away.

The strongman pulled a heavy knife from his leg sheath, cocked his arm and released. The blade whipped through the air and struck the deer directly behind its law bone, instantly severing both its jugular vein and carotid artery. The deer shivered once and then dropped dead.

The two men gutted and dressed it where it had fallen. Then Nathaniel cut down a sturdy pole of wood, spitted the deer on it and carried it over his shoulder as the headed back to the camp.

Back at the laager, as the sun went down, Nathaniel constructed two tripods from sturdy sticks lashed together with strips of bark, then he put one each side of the fire and lay the spitted deer over it.

Meanwhile Gramma had put on a pot of wild carrots and the girls had searched the trucks. Adalyn and Janeka had found two cajon drums. Basic wooden boxes with a sound hole and a snare. One sat on them like a stool and played by beating the front of the box with an open hand.

While the deer sizzled away on the spit the two girls beat out a rhythm. They started simple and soft, almost jazzy, and then segued into a more primal beat.

Jamaican Obeah underpinned by the savage cadence of North Africa. Mysterious and demanding.

Gramma joined in, chanting on every second beat. 'Hey-ah! Hey-ah! Hey-ah!'

Tad and Milly started to clap a counter rhythm, jagged and syncopated.

Nathaniel felt shivers run up and down his spine. Sweat poured down his back as he felt the spirit of the ancient music fill his soul. He tried to stop it but it demanded his attention. Insisting on him. His hair stood on end and power flowed into him. He felt like he was going to explode. His skin felt taut as a drum skin. Tiny flickers of blue fire sparkled all over his body. And the beat went on.

He stood up, threw his arms wide and howled at the heavens. Massive bolts of lightning leapt from his fingers and crashed against the sky. The sound of thunder rolled across the land and the smell of ozone filled the air.

The lightning formed a ball of iridescent blue fire that hovered for a while and then went crashing into the nearby forest, shattering trees and causing a vast swathe of fiery destruction.

The Forever Man fell to the floor and lay still. As still as death. His clothes were smoldering and his face was a pale as a full moon.

Once again, the night became still.

And far away an owl hooted as it searched for its mate.

Chapter 18

Nathaniel's consciousness came rushing back. A tidal wave of senses assailed him and he almost passed out again.

He glanced quickly around. He was seated on a horse on top of a small hill.

On his left stood another horse. Mounted on it, a man dressed in a grubby white tunic and robe. A druid. On his right, another four horses and a man holding a long brass horn. They were all dressed in great kilts, the tartan weave wrapped around their torsos as well as their hips. On each of their backs was a sheathed double-handed broadsword, in a shoulder scabbard. Hanging from each saddle, a large wooden quiver that held six heavy throwing spears.

The marine checked himself out. Suit of armor made from recycled car parts. Battle-axe. Fur cloak.

'Right,' he said quietly. 'Another one of those dreams.'

The druid shook his head. 'No dream, my lord. This is real.'

'But last time wasn't,' argued Nathaniel.

The druid pointed at the scar on the back of the marine's hand. 'Real enough to bleed.'

Nathaniel had no answer to that.

'Fair enough. Why am I here?'

The druid raised an eyebrow. 'Because you are. Because you always have been. This is the battle of Cunwarden. You are about to lead the tribe against the Romans from fort Cunwarden on Hadrian's Wall.'

Nathaniel cast his eyes over the terrain. On his far right, some two hundred yards away, stood around 200 cavalrymen, dressed in kilts and armed as were the men next to him. At the foot of the hill stood 100 archers, arrayed in two ranks of fifty. In front of them, 300 tribesmen armed with axes or broadswords. Some had shields. Many, however, had no armor whatsoever and many were actually completely naked. Stripped for battle, their bodies covered with intricate blue tattoos.

And opposite them, some 500 yards away, stood the might of the Romans. The marine did a quick calculation and figured that there were in excess of 3000 of them. Odds of 5 to 1 against. Not good.

The Romans had divided their troops into three groups of 1000. The 100 were further divided into 10 groups of 100, or a century. Each century had formed up into a testudo, or tortoise, their shields held high and overlapping, front ranks shields facing forward. Basically, a lightly armored troop carrier.

Nathaniel turned to the man on his right.

'Hey, dude. What's your name?'

'I am chief Cornavi, lord Degeo,' he then gestured at the other three men 'Chief Damnon, chief Maelon and chief Vericone. We live but to serve you, my lord Degeo.'

Nathaniel turned back to the druid. 'Lord Degeo?'

'Degeo. It means, forever or eternal. You are the eternal lord. The Forever Man.'

'Okay,' said Nathaniel. 'We can talk about that later. Cornavi, where are the Roman cavalry?'

'They have none, my lord. They keep horses for fast communication but that is all.'

'Reserves?'

'No, lord. What you see is what you get. The Romans are confident of crushing us utterly. They see no need to keep any troops in reserve.'

The marine stared at the array of Roman troops and thought hard.

'What about archers?'

'There are some manning the actual wall, lord. Perhaps fifty.'

'So, said the marine. 'Their plan is to simply walk towards us and crush us with their superior numbers. Not the most sophisticated of tactics.'

'They are doing that on purpose, lord. They seek to intimidate and insult us. They want to show that we, mere tribesmen, are unworthy of tactics.'

The marine smiled. 'Good. Now, here is what we shall do.'

He raised his voice so that the other chiefs could all hear him.

When he was finished the chiefs drew their swords and clashed them together.

'Oorah!'

And then they galloped off to the places that the marine had appointed them, ready to institute lord Degeo's battle plan. Three of the chiefs rode to the gathering of the tribesmen and the third, Cornavi, rode to the massed cavalry, but first he stopped by the archers and relayed their instructions. Then they waited for the call of the horn.

Nathaniel waited for the Romans to move first and, after about an hours wait, they did. Their testudo formations walked slowly forward, being careful to maintain their structure as they marched over the broken ground.

As per the marine's instructions the tribesmen broke into three groups of 100. One for each Roman cohort marching towards them. The two groups closest to Nathaniel began to retreat at the same pace that the

Romans advanced. The third group, however, stood firm.

The marine gave the horn blower a nod and he let out a long blast. "Ooo-reee!"

Immediately the archers bent their bows and fired at the third Roman cohort. They worked as swiftly as they could and, within seconds, the hail of steel tipped death rained down on the Roman testudo. Two, three, four and then five hundred arrows. Most stuck directly into the raised shields but many either penetrated or plunged between the gaps. Men fell, wounded, to the floor but the well-disciplined Roman machine simply trampled over them and continued the advance.

But, at the same time that the archers had begun to unleash their arrow storm, the cavalry had initiated a charge. They thundered down on the third cohort and the sound of 800 hooves shook the very ground. At the last moment, the cavalry wheeled away. But not before every man had unleashed a heavy spear into the formation. Unlike the lightweight arrows, the spears were massive heavy weapons. A foot of sharpened steel blade affixed to the top of a five-foot oaken shaft. The whole thing weighed in at over twenty pounds so, even un-bladed, it would have wreaked havoc. As it happened, 200 sharpened, heavyweight projectiles struck the testudo at once, causing it to instantly lose its shape. As it did so, more arrows found their way through, adding to the deaths and confusion. Then the cavalry unleashed their next spears.

The testudo ground to a halt.

The horn blew again. Twice. Ooo-reee! Ooo-reee!

And the first group of tribesmen, led by chief Damnon, charged the Roman cohort.

The Roman soldier is, by far and away, the best warrior when it comes to disciplined formation battle. They march forward behind the protection of their shield wall and, every now and then, on command, they part the wall, stab through using their short stabbing swords and then continue. Riding roughshod over all of their enemies.

Nathaniel knew that he had to break the formation. And the marine also knew that, once the fight turned into a mêlée then there was no possible way that a Roman soldier with a tiny 12-inch blade could compete against a berserker wielding a massive 40 or even 50-inch blade.

The group of tribesmen struck the Romans like a tsunami, smashing into them and hacking them to pieces.

Meanwhile, the cavalry and the archers were doing the same thing to the next cohort, with just as much success.

The final cohort, however, had reacted with typical Roman discipline and training and had reformed the testudo into a square with the commander and the standard bearer in the center. The cavalry threw their spears and the archers unleashed their shafts, but a square is more fluid than a testudo and it did not have to move. The soldiers used their shields to fend off the missiles and they waited for the tribesmen to charge, their shields locked together.

The running tribesmen hit the shield wall hard and met with death as the Romans parted the wall, thrust and closed. A score of tribesmen lay dead or wounded. But it was not in their nature to stop and, again and again they threw themselves at the impenetrable wall of steel. They could not get past it. Instead they merely flowed around it, like water around a rock. More of them dying on each pass.

Eventually the marine could stand no more. He dragged his axe from his belt, hammered his heels into his horse's sides and galloped down the hill at top speed, heading straight towards the square.

Knowing that he would be unable to force the horse to actually charge into the square he simply turned it at the last possible moment and leapt as hard as he could. Launching himself from the back of the galloping animal, through the air and into the middle of the square.

He rolled to his feet and immediately swung his axe, decapitating the commander. He leapt over the dead body and struck the standard bearer in the chest, splintering his bronze armor and slashing through his heart. He then grabbed the standard before it fell and held it above his head.

'Oorah!' He screamed. 'Oorah! For the corps and the good old USA.'

Then he pegged the standard into the turf and readied himself.

Without their commander, and with an enemy inside the formation holding their standard, the square lost its integrity as Romans broke rank in order to attack the marine.

They surged over him and he fought back like a maniacal dervish. Screaming the marine battle cry as he cut and parried. Blood flowed in rivulets, both the enemies and his own. A sword laid open the flesh from his right eye to his cheek and it flapped like a wet rag as he moved, but his armor prevented any mortal wounds and, after a mere five minuets, that felt like five days, his tribesmen had fought through to him.

Cornavi was the first and he threw himself in front of Nathaniel, swinging his broadsword in massive, cleaving arcs.

'My lord,' he shouted. 'I am here for you. Stand back.'

Two more tribesmen stood at Nathaniel's back and then another, and another.

Exhausted, the marine stopped fighting and merely leant on the shaft of his axe, panting and watching as the rough clad tribesmen slaughtered the Romans to the very last man.

After the slaughter and the looting of the bodies, the tribesmen attacked the wall itself. Using long poles cut from the forest, they levered blocks of stones out and then dragged them free until there was a twenty-yard breach in the wall.

Chief Cornavi explained to Nathaniel that they did this more for symbolic than for practical reasons. They had no wish to go south of the wall; they merely wanted to show the Romans that, if they had wanted to, then they could have.

***

That evening the clans gathered at chief Carnovi's village. Rude wood and daub huts surrounding a central cattle enclosure. Built on a hill, next to a stream. A wooden palisade enclosed tee entire village. Fields of crops lay outside; potatoes, turnips, beets and carrots.

Huge mastiff-type dogs roamed freely. However, the moment that Nathaniel arrived six of the vast animals crowded around him and followed him wherever he went, growling if anyone else got too close without Nathaniel's permission. The marine didn't discourage them as he was in a strange place and they gave him time to think.

The womenfolk, confident of the men's victory, had already prepared a feast. Long fires with many lambs rotating on spits above them. Long strips of leather joined the ten or so spits together onto one master cog that was attached to one of the massive dogs. The dog then walked in a prescribed circle, turning the meat so that it cooked evenly.

Tubs of sweet smelling mead were placed on the center of sturdy wooden tables and large wooden mugs were distributed to all. The mead was served by simply dunking your mug into the tub and helping yourself.

Before the festivities began, Nathaniel was taken to one side by one of the women. Her name was Gwencalon. She was tall for a woman, and muscular. Her hair a straw-yellow blond and her eyes a deep loch-blue, almost black. Her lips seemed to be set in a permanent slight smile, as if mocking the world. Laughing at it, not with it.

She sat Nathaniel down on a three legged stool and, using a cloth and water, cleaned out his facial wound. Then she sewed the flap closed, pulling it tight with four loops of coarse black gut. Afterwards she slapped on a poultice that smelled like urine.

Nathaniel choked.

'What the hell,' he said. 'Smells like piss.'

She laughed. Her laughter was as deep and husky as her speaking voice.

'Of course it does, my lord,' she said. 'For it is sheep's urine boiled down to form a paste. Without it, you would still heal but the scar would be a terrible blight on your sweet face.'

Then she wrapped a bandage around him, covering his nose and cheek but leaving his eyes free.

'Come, my lord,' she said. 'It is time for the brave men to feast.'

'And what about you?' Asked the marine.

Gwencalon lowered her eyes. 'Oh no, lord Degeo; it would not be seemly for a mere woman to sit with the warriors. We may forget our place.'

Again, Nathaniel noticed the mocking half-smile.

'What if I wanted you to sit with me?' He asked

Gwencalon's eyes flew open in genuine shock. 'No, my lord. Such a break with tradition would not do. Please, lord, do not even mention it.'

Nathaniel could see that she was truly worried.

'Okay,' he said. 'I won't. But if I want to see you again?'

The maid looked at him with what appeared to be genuine puzzlement. 'You are lord Degeo. You are The Forever Man. If thee finds want of me then thy wish is my command. Order and I shall be there.'

The marine raised an eyebrow. 'But would you want to be there?'

'If thy commands it, lord.'

Nathaniel shook his head. 'Whatever. Show me the way.'

The girl led Nathaniel through the small maze of huts and to the central open area next to the paddock. He was seated at the head table; on his right hand side sat chief Cornavi. His long beard, braided for the battle, had been combed free, as had his hair. The beard flowed to his chest and his raven hair lay down his back like a fur coat. On Nathaniel's left sat the druid. Clean-shaven, still dressed in his grubby white robe.

A mug of mead was put down in front of the marine and the chief stood up.

'We thank the gods fon r the return of our lord. Degeo Fear. The Forever Man.'

As one the tribe stood up and cheered.

Then the chief sat down and all waited in an expectant hush.

Eventually the druid leaned over and whispered. 'My lord, they are waiting for a speech.'

The marine, who had absolutely no idea what he was going to say, stood up and wracked his brain for something appropriate. Eventually he decided to simply throw together a few sound bites from famous speeches that he remembered.

'May the lightning of your glory be seen and the thunders of your onset heard from east to west. And let the Romans know, we shall fight them on the seas and oceans, we shall defend our land, whatever the cost may be. We shall fight on the beaches, we shall fight on the wall, we shall fight in the fields and in the streets, we shall fight in the hills; we shall never surrender.

Because we say, is life so dear or peace so sweet, as to be purchased at the price of chains and slavery? No – I forbid it, Almighty Gods! I know not what course others may take, but as for me, give me liberty or give me death! Oorah!'

The tribesmen erupted.

'Oorah! Oorah! Oorah!'

Nathaniel sat down.

'Well spoken, my lord,' said the druid. 'You are a great orator. You always have been.'

'Yeah,' said Nathaniel. 'You, Winston Churchill and I.'

'I'm sorry, lord?'

'Nothing. Hold on. What did you mean, I have always been. This is the first time that I have been here.'

'Quite the contrary, my lord,' denied the druid. 'You are oft here. That is why you are so well known. You are the clan lord. All seeing. All knowing. Forever being.'

Nathaniel shook his head. 'I have never been here before. I would know.'

The druid nodded. 'True. At this point in your life you have never been here. But at a later point you will have been here before. We know because you told us that you would lead us to a great victory against overwhelming odds at the battle of Cunwarden. And the only reason that you knew what would be, is that you had already done what had yet to be done.'

'Doesn't make sense,' argued Nathaniel.

'You are immortal,' said the druid.

'So?'

'Immortality works both ways, lord. The Forever Man is forever. Always was and always will be. Just, not yet.'

'What do I call you, druid?'

The druid smiled. 'I believe that you simply call me priest, or druid. Sometimes, dude. I am not sure what the last form of address means.'

'Fine, priest. How long do I normally stay?'

'Sometimes hours,' answered the druid. 'Sometimes for days. Once, for over a year.'

'Do you know how long I am staying this time?'

The druid nodded. 'Yes, lord. You told me the last time that you were here. You said that you would want to know.'

'Really?' Said Nathaniel in amazement. 'Well then, the next time I'm here, before I'm here now, well, I'd better remember to tell you to tell me.'

Most definitely, my lord.'

'Cool, dude. Now, how long.'

'You leave during the night, my lord. You had to, as your physical body is still in another time and place and it is dying.'

'I can't die,' said Nathaniel. 'Remember, the whole immortal thing.'

'Who says that immortality requires a body?' Asked the druid.

The marine stared at the priest for a while.

'Dude,' he said. 'Could it be that you are being deliberately obtuse?'

The druid smiled. 'Sorry, my lord. I couldn't help myself. Forgive me. Whenever you refer to me as, dude, it brings out my worst.'

'Well don't screw with The Forever Man,' said Nathaniel. 'Answer me. How can I die? I am immortal.'

The druid blanched. 'I am sorry, my lord Degeo. It was not my intention to play fornication upon you. In answer to your question, I am not completely sure. You are in two places at the same time. I think, in those circumstances, one of you can die. I have no idea what the ramifications of that death would be.'

'How do I go back?'

The druid shook his head. 'Sorry, my lord. You simply disappear.'

Nathaniel downed his mug of mead.

'Fine. Look, priest, I'm exhausted. I need sleep. Get someone to show me to my digs and I'll catch some nap time.'

The druid clapped his hands and Gwencalon appeared.

'You summoned, high borne one,' she said to the druid.

'Yes. Take lord Degeo to his hut and help him to rest.'

The tall girl beckoned to the marine who stood and followed her. They walked to the largest hut in the village. She led the way, ducking through the small open front entrance. Inside was a single large room. The thatch roof was steeply pitched and in the center was a fire, the smoke drifting lazily through a hole in the middle of the thatch ceiling. To the one side of the fire was a mountain of sleek, soft furs, piled high and wide.

Nathaniel pulled off his armor with a sigh of relief and snuggled into the pile of warmth and softness, pulling one of the furs over him.

Gwencalon unclipped the brooch that held up her tunic and let the green shift flow to the floor. She was naked underneath and her body was hard and rounded. The firelight reflected off her erect nipples and cast her womanhood into mysterious shadow.

With her ever-present half-smile on her lips she pulled back the fur that covered The Forever Man.

To discover that he was no longer there.

Chapter 19

Aapep Nu stood at the window, his back to the room, ignoring the human maid who was cleaning his rooms.

Aapep was a lower order Fair-Folk mage. And, since the incident at the village of Pennance and the following death of the human Baker brothers, he had been sent to the Pennance garrison in order to ensure that the humans were kept under control.

This had not been as easy as he had thought it would be. Firstly, the thin skins did not actually do anything flagrantly wrong. They were more passive-aggressive as opposed to simply aggressive. They would deliberately stand in the way when one of the Fair-Folk or their minions would seek to walk a path. They would light bonfires and cover them with noxious weeds whenever the wind blew over the garrison and then, when asked to put the fires out, they would simply walk away. A group of young boys had been caught urinating in the garrison water tanks. They had been birched as punishment but had refused to apologize.

Of course they could be glamoured, and Aapep did make full use of his glamoring powers that could affect both the human's perception and the way that they behaved. However, it was very tiring and, unlike they had first thought, the thin skins were actually fairly resistant to the process. It appeared that humans tended to find glamoring acceptable, only if they essentially agreed with what was happening in the first place. So, if you were well liked, a small amount of glamour would ensure that you were extremely well liked. However, if they were suspicious of you, then it took an inordinate amount of power to bend their will. They were an obstinate and irrational race, full of unnecessary feelings and devoid of logic.

Aapep turned from the window and walked to his desk where he sat staring at the female human. Her name was Debbie and she was sixteen earth years old. Lank, mousy hair. Hazel eyes. Thin. Aapep had no idea if she was considered attractive or not. To him she looked the same as all of them. Like the constructs that the Fair-Folk bred as workers, she was a pale color, built on a similar skeletal structure and of similar strength. But it was there that the similarities ended.

Unlike any of the Fair-Folk's breedings, the humans had been granted emotion. Constructs felt no emotions at all. Orcs and goblins were capable of only the most rudimentary. As a result the Orcs, the Goblins and the constructs felt no fear, no curiosity. They had no need to question, and they never did.

The Fair-Folk, on the other hand, did experience emotions. They simply kept them well under control. But when they were in front of the thin skins there was no need for such control. In fact, quite the opposite. Many of the younger Fair-Folk, like Aapep who had only recently had his bicentennial celebration, had taken to openly glamoring humans in order to bring on excesses of emotional responses and then reveling in their after effects. Feeding on their fear and their pain, like psychic vampires. Imbibers of the raw emotions that the thin skins experienced when under the extreme duress of being physically glamoured.

They had tried joy and love, but the frisson that one experienced from these warm and fuzzy emotions were nothing like the high that one could experience by glamoring a subject into abject gibbering terror and then soaking up their emotion. It was indescribably delicious.

And, afterwards, if you released them from the glamour in the correct way, they forgot all about it and went on their way. Only to return for more pleasure enhancing mental torture when next summoned.

'Debbie, child,' he called her over to her. 'Come here.'

The teenager walked over to stand in front of the small gray alien that she saw as a tall, blonde, strikingly handsome man.

Aapep started by drawing in some of the power of the life-light and using it to freeze Debbie to the spot. Then he forced her mind open and thrust himself in, pushing deep into the layers of her consciousness. And there he found it, locked away in some dark, windowless room. Heights. She was terrified of heights.

He drew in a little more power…and tweaked.

'No!' Debbie screamed. She looked down. She saw that she was balanced on the top of a tall spire. A cathedral. Hundreds of feet below, people scuttled like insects. Birds flew below her. Wisps of cloud caressed her face.

She cried out again. A formless sound of nightmares. A lowing, mooing sob of terror.

'Please help me,' she called out to no one.

Aapep allowed the teenager to see him. Standing in front of her. It made no logical sense but she was now in a dreamlike state of pure glamour.

'I am here, child,' he said.

'Help me, sir.'

'Of course.' Aapep held out his hand. 'Take my hand, child. Take my hand and I shall carry you to safety.'

Debbie shook her head. Tears poured down her face. 'I'm scared.'

'No need, child. I shall save you. Trust me.'

Aapep stretched towards her.

She leaned forward.

And Aapep snatched his hand back.

She fell. In reality, a short, one second stumble to the floor.

But, in her new reality, a fall of minutes.

Twice Aapep had to use the life-light to restart the girl's terror-stilled heart as she fell. And then once again when she hit the ground.

Aapep's breath came in shuddering gasps as he sank to his knees. Sweat poured from his rubbery skin and soaked into his loincloth. He squeezed his eyes tightly shut and waited for the waves of the thin skin's delicious, unfettered terror to finish washing over him.

Finally, he rose unsteadily to his feet and gave Debbie a mental nudge.

The young girl stood up and swayed in place for a while.

Eventually she spoke.

'Can I do anything for you, sir?'

Aapep shook his head.

'Go,' he said. 'I will send for you if I need you.'

Debbie nodded and left the room. It was as if all had never happened. She was totally unaffected by her glamoring.

However, deep inside the tissue of her brain a large blood vessel that had been weakened by the massive cerebral trauma started to expand like a balloon, causing a large aneurysm. That midnight, whilst Debbie was asleep, the aneurysm burst.

She never awoke from her slumber.

Chapter 20

Both Adalyn and Janeka rushed forward in an attempt to grab Nathaniel before he hit the ground but they were too late.

Gramma Higgins waddled over and knelt down next to the prone marine, feeling at his neck for a pulse.

'He's alive,' she said. 'Though he look no better than a corpse.'

'What the hell was that?' Exclaimed Tad. 'I mean, is it just me or did he just create a lightning storm?' He gestured towards the burning tract of forest. 'Did Nate just do that?'

Gramma nodded. 'It appears dat he jus did. Now stop yo fussin and fetch me a blanket or sumat.'

Milly ran off and returned with one of Nathaniel's furs.

'Thank you, child,' said Gramma, as she covered the marine.

The little girl lay down on the ground next to Nathaniel, pulled her own fur cloak over both of them and then she snuggled up close to keep him warm.

'Dat's good, Milly,' approved Gramma. 'Keep him warm. He be in some sort of shock right now and we don't want him dying on us.'

Milly smiled. 'Don't worry, Gramma,' she assured. 'Nate can't die.'

'Thas right, child,' said Gramma. 'You think positive. Good.'

This time Milly actually laughed. 'No, Gramma. I mean it. Nate cannot die. A few days ago, I saw him get shot in the heart by some bad men with big guns and he fell down, all blood and terrible stuff. Then the bad men stole all of his clothes and left him lying in the snow. Two days later he found me and rescued me. And he was fine.'

'They probably jus nicked him, sweetheart,' said Gramma.

'No,' argued Milly; 'They hit him. Right in the middle of the chest. Twice. I was there and I saw it and two days later he was fine. He cannot die.'

Not wanting to belittle the girl's story but keen to get to the bottom of it, Gramma leaned over and pulled the furs away from Nathaniel's chest.

And there, easily visible in the firelight, were two coin sized pink scars. Newly healed. She turned him slightly so that she could see his back and, sure enough, in the corresponding areas, were two large exit scars. Perhaps the size of small teacups. Also newly healed. Gramma pulled the furs back up and tucked them tight around the marine.

'She speaks the truth,' she said. Her voice barely above a whisper.

'Told you so,' said Milly.

'So,' said Tad. 'We have ourselves an immortal ex-marine who can create his own firestorms.'

Suddenly Milly screamed.

Tad jumped back. 'What?'

The little girl pointed at Nathaniel's face. On his right side a huge gash appeared, flaying the flesh from the side of his face. The marine's body jerked slightly and Gramma pulled back the furs to reveal more cuts opening on his upper neck and forearms. None of them, however, bled. It was if someone had slashed open a week old corpse.

'What do we do now?' Asked Tad, his voice close to hysteria.

Gramma shook her head. 'Nothing. We keep him warm. That's it. Nothing else that we can do. Dis be way beyond our knowledge of tings.'

Milly was crying quietly. Adalyn stroked her hair. 'Don't worry. You said he can't die.'

Milly nodded. 'But he can still feel. And something has chopped his face up.'

There was no answer so they all simply sat in vigilance around the comatose body. Watching. Waiting. Silent.

Milly, Adalyn and Janeka eventually fell asleep. Tad and Gramma sat awake.

The son rose, heavy, gray and ineffectual. A light snow started to fall. Tad erected a small tent over the marine to keep him dry.

They waited.

'Look,' said Tad as he pointed at the marine's face.

Both Gramma and he stared and, as they did, the horrendous scar slowly knitted itself together, leaving a thin pink line. The other visible scars also closed, some leaving hardly a sign of their existence.

Milly woke up, stretched, ran her fingers over Nathaniel's scar and smiled.

An hour later the marine woke up.

He looked around him, taking in the familiar surrounds and said.

'Cool. Home again.'

Chapter 21

The one that they all called G-Man swung his leg hard. The toe of the Doc Marten boot struck Harry in the chest, the sound like an axe chopping wood. The burly farmer fell backwards and smashed his head on the wall.

There was no way that could fight back. His arms were tied behind his back and his legs had been taped together with duct tape. And, even if he had been free to retaliate, he could not. The newcomers had his wife and his two daughters and he knew that they would harm them if he tried anything. So he didn't. He merely absorbed their punishment and waited.

'You know something, Harry?' Asked G-Man. 'You are one sorry asshole. Really, who did you think that you were? Jesus. Gandhi. You wanted to lead. You wanted to be the king, just like any one else. Admit it, Harry. You wanted to be the boss.'

Harry shook his head. 'No, G-Man. I simply wanted to help. People were dying. I wanted to help.'

'Well you have,' said G-Man. 'You helped us.'

More kicks were delivered. Savage, crunching blows.

Harry didn't even attempt to stay conscious as the blows rained down on him. He knew that there was no humiliation in what was happening to him. He had done the right thing. He just hoped that they didn't harm Ann and the two girls.

Eventually G-Man got bored of kicking an inanimate object and he skulked off, followed by his two main sidekicks, Jonno and Ratman. G-Man stood around six foot. A long slab of a face, like a sallow tombstone. Black hair slicked back close to his skull to reveal a widows peak. Green eyes, bushy eyebrows and a permanently disappointed expression.

All three men were armed with sawn-off shotguns and daggers. Ratman, a 300-pound gorilla of a man, also carried a three-foot long sledgehammer with a fifteen-pound head. He called the hammer "Daisy" and had used it as a weapon many times. He made a point of never cleaning it afterwards. The bits of bone, gristle and hair embedded in the layers of dried blood were mute testimony to that. Ratman, who had gained his nickname after eating a live rat, claimed that the grisly state of the hammer's head intimidated people. He was correct.

The three men headed back to the main farmhouse. The same house that had, up until three days ago, when G-Man and his cohorts had arrived, been farmer Harry's house.

They passed the neat rows of different size and color tents pitched outside the house. Outdoor latrines had been dug about one hundred yards from the tents and a six foot barbed wire fence surrounded the living enclave.

Outside the enclave was a working farm. Crops, mainly potatoes, were being planted and reaped as well as swedes and turnips. Hardy root crops that could withstand the cold. Dairy cattle and horses were stabled inside the secure enclave.

When the pulse had first hit, Harry, a well-known farmer in the area, had reacted quickly. He had saddled up his horse and visited all of his neighbors, convincing them to pack up and come to his farm, as it was the biggest in the area.

Within two weeks the people had fenced in the secure area, dug a well and started all of the routines necessary to subsist and prosper.

Initially there had been thirty of them. However, they had formed a four-man committee and had decided that small groups of three people, two men and one woman, would saddle up and ride forth to seek out other people in distress. At least one group set out each day, roaming far and wide. By the end of the first month there were over one hundred people living at Harry's farm and another family arrived every two or three days.

Harry, his wife and his two daughters, lived in a tent, as did all of the other families. They had given the farmhouse over as a clinic, a kitchen and a common area. Some rooms held card games, others prepared pickles and jams and still more rooms were set aside for the elderly and infirm.

Harry's farm was an oasis of calm. A haven of kindness and sanity in a world of madness. And, as such, it was doomed to fail.

G-Man and his buddies had arrived four days ago and had simply taken over. There were twenty-two of them. All armed with a mixture of shotguns, rifles, crossbows and edged weapons.

Harry and his people had welcomed them with open arms and, within hours, three of them were dead and G-Man had raped one of the teenagers. The two people that had died were both young men who had tried to stop the rape. It was not that G-Man and his compadres were that much stronger than everyone on Harry's farm. It was not that the people on Harry's farm were not brave enough. It was simply that G-Man and his buddies' were of a type. Bottom feeders.

Inherently vicious and paranoid. The results of a benefits culture that had not done an honest day's work for over three generations. A culture of entitlement that had resulted in the selective interbreeding of the lowest of the low. They were, quite simply, consumers and destroyers.

G-Man led the way to the main house that had been turned into his residence since the takeover. The elderly and infirm had been relegated to tents. As had the cooking facilities.

Jonno and Ratman shared the house with G-Man and the other nineteen vagabonds had requisitioned the biggest tents for themselves.

The gentle commune had degenerated into a caricature of a Wild West town with G-Man as the villain.

But wherever we find a villain in such stories, we also find a tall, dark, stranger that rides into town.

Chapter 22

Sharing someone's terror and enhanced emotional highs is exhilarating. It is exciting. It is both mind expanding and conscious altering.

However, it is also very addictive, as Aapep was in the process of finding out. To a species that had never been exposed to the radical highs and lows of humanities emotional states, mind melding with the thin skin's terror enhanced minds was the equivalent of Fair-Folk crack cocaine.

The Fair-Folk lived very long lives. An average of over four hundred earth years. With their massive cerebrums, they all had what humans would refer to as eidetic, or photographic memories. As well as this, they had an ability to pass on their memories, or at least an almost exact facsimile. As a result, most Fair-Folk carried with them the sum total of their entire race's memories. In all that time, Aapep could not recall anyone experiencing such hedonistic surfeits of emotion as he had been experiencing over the last couple of weeks.

Then, quite by chance, he had discovered the mother-lode. One of the thin skin serving girls had brought her child with her. She had left the child, a nine year old, in Aapep's living area while she had gone to fetch cleaning rags and polishing wax. Aapep had taken the opportunity to glamour the child into absolute terror and the resultant waves of emotion were the most intense that he had ever experienced. Pure and unadulterated by logic or learning, the child's terror was as clear and sharp as a blade.

And now all else felt feeble. As if a cloud had passed in front of the light of his emotions and left him in a fog of dull, unrelenting normalness.

Unfortunately, the child had suffered from a terminal heart attack while under the influence and it had died. When the mother returned Aapep had glamoured her as well, not because he needed another fix, he had been fully sated by the child. He did the woman merely to overtax her cerebral system and cause her death. Then he had contacted Orc sergeant Gog via mental telepathy and called him to his chambers.

Gog had cleaned up, disposing of the bodies and ensuring no one knew that the girl had been in the camp. Simply another couple of thin skins that had disappeared

Aapep stared out of the window. Outside the main gates three boys played. One, a little larger than the other two, appeared to be in charge. His face was covered in gray river mud and he held a wooden broadsword and a round wooden buckler. It was obvious, even to Aapep who had no real imagination, that the boy was playing the role of a battle Orc. The two other boys were probably thin skin vagabonds or thieves or such. The three of them raged back and forth killing each other over and over again. And then laughing and patting each other on the backs and starting again.

Aapep pulsed a message to Gog.

'Come.'

Within minutes the sergeant was knocking at the door.

'Enter,' commanded Aapep.

The battle Orc shambled in.

Aapep beckoned him over to the window and pointed at the three boys.

'The one with mud on his face. Bring him to me.'

Gog nodded and left, of to do his master's bidding.

Aapep sat down on his sofa and sipped at a sherbet. A human drink made from apple, ginger, orange and lemon. He concentrated on the glass and drew some of the heat from it. Condensation rolled down the sides. Delicious.

Outside the main gate, sergeant Gog shambled up to the three young boys at play. They immediately stopped and stood in a line. The bigger one threw a clumsy salute.

'Greetings, sergeant Gog,' he said. 'Tommy Tiernan, sir. Reporting for duty.'

Gog shook his head. 'No, human. You don't salute me. I am a sergeant. I work for a living. You salute officers. Also, just sergeant. Never, sir. Get it?'

Tommy and his friends nodded enthusiastically.

'Yes, sergeant,' said Tommy. 'How can we help you, sergeant?'

'You must go,' said Gog. 'You are no longer allowed to conduct your battle exercises here. Leave now.'

Tommy's face crumpled. 'Aaaah! Please, sergeant.'

Gog shook his head.

'No. Leave or you will be punished.' He raised a massive right claw and the boys scampered off.

The sergeant turned around and trudged back to Aapep's abode, knocked on the door and went in.

The Fair-Folk lord stared at him.

'Where is the boy?'

'Gone,' answered Gog.

'But I sent you to get him.'

Gog nodded. 'Yes.'

'So where is he, I ask again.'

'Gone.'

'Sergeant Gog. Are you deliberately disobeying an order?'

Gog, who had never actually come across the concept of disobedience before, had to think before he answered.

'Yes, sir. I believe that I am.'

Aapep stood up, drew power in, and lashed out like a frustrated child. A bolt of physic energy flashed across the room and struck Gog in the chest, burning through his leather breastplate and scorching his skin.

'Go and get the boy for me!' Screamed Aapep.

Gog shook his head.

Aapep struck again. This time with more vigor. The bolt lashed across Gog's face, ripping the flesh from its right side and exposing the bone. And, although the pain must have been immense, the Orc did not even flinch.

'Why?' Screamed Aapep. 'Why?'

Again the Orc thought. Eventually he spoke.

'Because he waved to me.'

'And because of this you are prepared to die?'

Again, Gog's thought process stumbled along unfamiliar pathways until he reached a conclusion.

'Yes,' he replied. 'He is a...' The battle Orc paused for a while as his tongue tried to form an unfamiliar word. 'Friend.'

The next blast of psychic fire tore the head from Gog's shoulders and threw him out of the room.

Aapep screamed in frustration and then sank to his knees, overcome with humanlike feelings of anger that his alien mind was not psychologically geared to handle.

Chapter 23

G-Man lowered the binoculars.

'Looks like six of them. Riding two to a horse. Three women, couple of kids and a man. No worries. Let them come. The more the merrier.'

The small cavalcade of three horses drew closer, meandering down the hill and to the front gate of the farm. At all times they were covered by at least two of G-Man's men, rifles raised to shoulders.

They stopped twenty yards from G-Man and the adult male dismounted.

'Greetings,' he said. 'My name is Nathaniel Hogan. United States Marine Corps. These are my compadres. It's good to see human company. Could we bother you for some water? A place to bed down for the night?'

G-Man stared at Nathaniel for a while and then steeped forward, his face agrin, his hand held out.

The marine came forward to meet him and they shook hands.

'Welcome,' said G-Man. 'Welcome to Harry's Farm, a patch of paradise in a sea of desolation. Don't mind the boys with the guns, tough times call for radical methods.'

Nathaniel nodded his agreement and gestured to Gramma Higgins, Tad and the girls. They dismounted and introduced themselves to G-Man who managed to control his surprise when he saw that, what he had thought to be a child, was actually a small, muscle-bound young adult male in his early twenties.

'They call me G-Man,' he said to all. 'On account of that I look like G-Man from the video game, Half-Life.'

Nathaniel shrugged. 'Don't know it. Sorry.'

'No worries. Come, follow me.' G-Man set off into the encampment, four of his armed men walked with them. Nathaniel and his group followed, leading their horses.

'So, where do you hail from?'

'Here and there,' answered Nathaniel. 'I was posted at the American Embassy, London. Pulse hit. Came north. Met these people along the way.'

'We're a little more local stock,' said G-Man. 'Leeds mainly. After the world died we all got together, left the city and roamed about a bit until we found a place suitable. We came across this place. Harry's Farm. Basically run by a bunch of hippies. Pathetic. You know the type, equal rights for all, pro gay, pro feminist, pro bloody everything. So, we took over. Provided a bit of well needed discipline and structure.' G-Man glanced slyly across at Nathaniel, gauging his reaction.

The marine said nothing.

G-Man continued. 'We've got a spare tent. You'll all have to share. The rules around here are very simple. Rule one, if I tell you what to do, you do it. Rule two, if one of my men tells you what to do, they speak with my voice, so, refer to rule one. Rule three, if you don't like it then you are welcome to piss off. Unless I say that you can't, then refer to rule one again. Any infractions of the rules will be dealt with harshly. Any questions?'

The marine shook his head. 'You're the boss. Simple. No problem.'

G-Man smiled. 'Great. Here's the tent. Tie your horses to the rail. Water buckets and hay are there for them. You got four cots; I'll get another two sent up. Enjoy, we'll speak later, soldier boy.'

Nathaniel nodded.

G-Man and his entourage left.

Adalyn and Janeka started talking at the same time.

'What a horrible man,' said Janeka.

'Anti gay, anti equal rights, anti everything. A real piece of work,' agreed Adalyn.

'Dat a real bad man make his own Babylon here on da farm,' said Gramma. 'I think we spends da night and den we goes, quick as quick can be.'

'I agree, Gramma' said Tad. 'Wouldn't trust that smiley asshole further than I could throw him.'

'So, Nathaniel,' said Gramma. 'What we gonna do?'

The marine threw his saddlebag onto a cot and then sat down.

'Nothing.'

'Why?' Asked Tad. 'You trust this slime-ball?'

Nathaniel looked at the little man, his face impassive. But behind his green eyes a light crackled with fury. 'Trust him? The asshole called me a soldier.'

'So.'

'I am a Marine. Nobody calls me army. We stay. We stay and we see what the hell is going on around here. But keep frosty, people. No outbursts, no antagonizing the local pops and no arguments. Stay under the wire, keep your mouths closed and your eyes open.'

There was a general nodding of agreement.

'Right then,' continued the marine. 'Let's split up and do a recce. Gramma, you take the girls and Tad and I will go our own way. Chat to whomever you can, but be subtle. See you all back here before sundown.'

They all left the tent, the girls headed right and Nathaniel and Tad broke left.

***

'I'm not sure, G-Man,' said Jonno. 'I don't like the marine. There's something about him. Can't quite put my finger on it.'

'Naw,' disagreed G-Man. 'It's just because he's a Yankee Doodle Dandy. He's just like everybody else, looking for a place to stay. Crapping themselves in the dark every night. We provide food, security and in return all we ask for is that they do as they are told.'

Jonno shook his head. 'I dunno. These marines are hard asses. I heard that they don't take crap from nobody.'

'You want I should introduce him to Daisy, boss,' rumbled Ratman as he picked up his sledgehammer.

'No. Leave him alone. Trust me, I have a feeling that the American could turn out to be quite an asset. Watch, wait and see.'

***

Two more cots had been delivered to the tent and each person in the group sat on their own cot and partook of the evening meal. It was filling but basic. Meat gruel made from oats and lamb and spinach.

There was a day when someone like Milly might have complained if given a watery porridge with meat and greens in but, in the new world, it was considered by all to be a hearty meal.

In fact, Nathaniel was wondering how many picky eaters, children who were "allergic" to fish, skinny teenage girls "allergic" to gluten, had now buckled down and simply ate what they were given. He wondered how many had died from it. And how many had been miraculously cured when they discovered that they had never actually suffered from Coeliacs but rather from merely being spoiled self-absorbed assholes. He grinned to himself.

Gramma scraped her bowl with her spoon and then placed it on the floor next to her bed.

'There be bad stuff going on here, marine, bad stuff. We got to speak to some of de girls, mainly youngsters but some teenagers. It seems like G-Man's boys are given the pick of de girls whenever dey feel like it. In the beginning some of the men-folk they did complain. They were taken, nailed to the side of de barn and whipped. Now de girls go without a fight. Not willingly, but to prevent bloodshed. They'se good people. I think dat G-Man, he wasn't too far wrong when he called them hippies. All dey want is love and to live and let live. It's sad but, in this dark world of today, dat surely is a way to end up subjugated to some asshole like G-Man. Oh how dat be true.'

Nathaniel nodded. 'Well said, Gramma, well said. Tad and I spoke to the outlaws. There's about twenty of them. Lowlife scum. Not a professional amongst them. Petty thieves, job dodgers and benefit frauds. Tad and I could take them with both hands tied behind our backs and our shoelaces tied together. But there would be collateral damage. Stray bullets, wholesale slaughter. I've got to be a little subtler than I usually am. Subterfuge is called for. However, first things first. If any of the outlaws make any type of inappropriate move on you girls, you tell Tad or me. Then it be all, damn collateral damage and we'll slaughter the assholes. You understand?'

The girls nodded.

'Okay, Adalyn and Janeka, if anyone asks, say that you're my girls and I don't share. Right?'

Adalyn nodded but Janeka shook her head.

'Not happy, Janeka?' Asked Nathaniel.

'I wanna say that I'm Tad's girl,' she said, and she stood up and went and sat next to the little man.

The marine grinned. 'Fine, you're Tad's girl.'

Janeka smiled wide and Tad blushed crimson and stared at his feet.

'Adalyn,' continued Nathaniel with a grin. 'You happy or do you want to be Tad's girl as well?'

'I be your girl,' agreed Adalyn.

'Whose girl am I?' Asked Milly.

'You're my girl, sweetheart,' said Nathaniel. 'Everybody knows that.'

Milly ran over and gave the marine a kiss on the cheek. Then she went back to her bed, pulled her fur cloak over herself, and lay down.

'I be no one's girl,' said Gramma. 'But I can always live in hope dat one of those boys makes me an indecent proposal. Mm-hmm, I surely could show him a good time,' she cackled and slapped her knee.

'Gramma,' chided Janeka.

'Don't you Gramma me, young lady,' retorted the oldster. 'Least I not be pushing some poor young muscle-bound oaf into being my boyfriend. You watch her, young Tad, she be a mighty forward little girl. Mighty forward.'

Tad smiled wryly but said nothing.

And then Nathaniel told them all, in husky whispers, the plan that he had formulated. After they had discussed it and gone over it a few times, it was dark.

They all crawled into their cots and went to sleep. Their bodies tied to the rising and the setting of the sun like Dark Age peasants.

Chapter 24

Nathaniel and Tad walked over to the main farmhouse and greeted the two armed guards at the door.

'Hey,' said the marine. 'We need to see the boss. Is he in?'

'Hold on,' replied the one guard who turned and went inside. He returned a minute later. 'Come in. Boss will see you.'

He led the way down the corridor and into a large eat-in kitchen. A wood burning Coleman stove stood in the one corner. Coffee simmered in a large pot on top. The aroma assailed Nathaniel's nostrils like the smell of a beautiful woman and he stared at the pot with undisguised lust.

'Good morning, gentlemen,' greeted G-Man.

They both nodded.

'Sit,' continued the outlaw chief. 'Coffee?'

'I'd kill for coffee,' grunted Nathaniel. 'Black, please. No sugar.'

Tad shook his head. 'None for me,' he said. 'Caffeine makes me go mental.'

G-Man poured a large mug for Nathaniel, placed it on the kitchen table.

'Sit,' he repeated. 'And talk to me.'

The marine sipped at the coffee before he spoke.

'On our way here,' he started. 'We came across an encampment. Maybe ten people, no more. Seemed to be all male. We came across them just before nightfall and we stayed hidden just in case they were inhospitable. They had made a camp by laagering a number of trucks in a circle, fire and livestock in the middle. Stream close by. Tad and I sneaked up and did a bit of a recce. What we saw was interesting but the two of us couldn't take advantage of things. I have no idea how, or where, they came by them, but the group appeared to have at least two truckloads of fully automatic weapons. Cases of the new SA85 bullpup, L8A3 machine guns, grenades, claymore mines and tons of ammo. Looks like they might have ripped off a military column or base. They weren't military themselves. Just simple lowlife retards that had lucked out.'

G-Man nodded. 'Cool. So what?'

'Well,' continued Nathaniel. 'What arms have you got here? A couple of bolt-action rifles, a few shotguns, a handgun or two? Imagine if every one of your boys had an assault rifle capable of firing over 750 rounds a minute. Machine guns with 100 round disintegrating belts of ammo. Hand grenades capable of blowing up whole buildings. Boss, you would be unstoppable. Why settle for being boss of Harry's Farm? I know that you want to be more,' said Nathaniel. 'I can tell a leader when I see one. You could control the whole county. More, the whole northwest of the UK. Why be boss when you could be king?'

G-Man leaned back in his chair and attempted to look more like the sort of man who desired a kingdom as opposed to the lightweight petty criminal that he was.

'We don't know how to use those weapons,' he argued.

'But I do,' answered Nathaniel. 'That's my thing. I could train your boys up in a couple of weeks and then we would be unstoppable.'

'What's in it for you?' Asked G-Man.

'I want to be part of the inner circle,' answered the marine. 'Both Tad and I. We can help, we're both good with weapons and Tad has particularly good knife skills. We can oversee any new troops that you take on. We can help.'

G-Man steepled his hands in front of his face and thought for a while.

Then he nodded.

'I like it. So, how do we get these weapons?'

'Easy,' said Nathaniel. 'Tad and I take ten of your boys out late afternoon. We arrive at the camp just after dark. Sneak in, kill them and bring the weapons back. No worries.'

'That simple, you say?' Asked G-Man.

'Yep. They won't be expecting anything, they're amateurs. In, out, easy.'

'Okay,' agreed G-Man. But you take Jonno with you. I want someone that I know in charge, so you take your orders from him. And remember the rules? Jonno speaks with my voice, so you obey. Right?'

Both Tad and Nathaniel nodded. 'Right.'

***

They set out on horses that late afternoon. Nathaniel, Tad, Jonno and nine other men. Jonno carried a rifle, the others had shotguns. Nathaniel and Tad were armed only with their bladed weapons. Tad with his knives and the marine with his axe and two new razor-sharp knives that Tad had given him.

They ambled along in a column of two, Nathaniel taking a slightly longer route than necessary, as he wanted to make sure that they arrived when it was dark so that it was not immediately apparent that the camp was empty.

The sun set and, when they got closer, the marine told them to all dismount and tether their horses. Then they continued on foot.

As the laager of vehicles hove into view, the marine called them all together and explained his plan. They would split into three groups. Tad and three others, Nathaniel and five outlaws and then Jonno, providing cover with his rifle, and two assistants. 'Right, Jonno,' whispered the marine. 'You and your two boys stay here. Keep cover, no need for you to take a chance on getting hurt. I'll go right and Tad will go left. Once we're opposite each other I'll signal with an owl call and then Tad's group and my group slip in, cut throats and call you when it's done. Happy?'

Jonno nodded. 'Happy. Let's do it.'

They split up and started to crawl through the grass to their appointed positions. Nathaniel waited until they had crawled for over a hundred yards then he tapped one of the men on the shoulder and beckoned for him to stop crawling.

'What's your name?' He whispered.

'Jason.'

'Good,' said Nathaniel. 'Listen, Jason. Slight change of plan. I think that it'll be better off if we spread out a little. Come from them at all angles at once. Really use the element of surprise. Get it?'

Jason nodded.

'Fine,' continued the marine. 'You stay here and wait for the signal.' Nathaniel looked up to check and saw that the rest of the outlaws were still crawling and were now over fifty yards ahead. Carefully, he drew one of his knives and then he leaned over, as if to pat Jason on the shoulder. But instead he clamped his hand over the man's mouth and nose and then slit his throat from ear to ear. Jason's body jerked spasmodically for a few seconds and then went limp.

Nathaniel crawled quickly through the long grass to catch up with the other four outlaws. As soon as he caught up with the man at the back, he did the same thing, leaving another cooling corpse behind him.

But the third man turned as Nathaniel put his hand over his mouth and, instead of clamping over his face, his grip slid off and the man shouted and bit Nathaniel's thumb hard enough to bring blood welling to the surface.

The marine stabbed the man in the stomach and pushed up hard, attempting to reach his heart, but the blade wasn't long enough. Nathaniel pushed again and then his vision starred as the last outlaw in the group smashed the butt of his shotgun into Nathaniel's temple. The marine dragged the blade up as hard as he could, disemboweling the biter as he did. Then he spun around, grabbed the final outlaw by his neck and, with a heave of supercharged muscle, snapped his spine.

The marine then made a split second decision. He would have to rely on Tad taking care of his own business and he would have to neutralize Jonno. He picked up two of the fallen men's shotguns and, one in each hand, pointed them at the laager and pulled the triggers. Four shots boomed out across the landscape and four massive tongues of flame lit up the night.

Then he turned and ran as fast as he could back towards Jonno and his two men, unsheathing his axe as he moved.

'What the hell is happening?' Shouted Jonno.

'Everything's gone wrong,' replied Nathaniel as he approached. They were waiting for us. Everyone else is dead.'

'What? How?' Asked Jonno.

'I killed them,' said the marine as he swung left and right with his axe, decapitating the two men with Jonno.

He raised his axe high. Jonno fired and Nathaniel felt the bullet burn as it creased his ribs. Then the blade bit down and struck Jonno's head from his torso in a spectacular fountain of gore.

He spun and started to sprint towards Tad's side of the laager, cutting through the middle of it as he ran. He broached the circle and saw the little man standing against the bonnet of a truck. His face was covered in blood and he was smoking a cigarette. 'Took your time, didn't you,' said Tad as Nathaniel jerked to a stop, his chest heaving with the effort of sprinting so fast.

The marine pointed at the little man's face.

'Blood.'

'Yeah,' said Tad. 'I know. One of the bastards shot the top of my ear off. Doesn't half bleed, I tell you. And you?' He asked.

'And me what,' countered Nathaniel.

Tad pointed at the marine's side. It was covered in blood.

'Oh,' admitted Nathaniel. 'That. Got shot. Again. Should be alright by the time that we get back.'

Tad lit another cigarette and handed it over to the marine.

They stood in silence for a while and smoked.

Above them the night sky coruscated with the color of the aurora borealis.

Far away a fox barked.

And Tad told the marine his story. Starting with the death of mister Burnaby, and then Zorba, Adelpha, the bearded fat lady with the poison mushrooms. By the time that Tad got to the five clowns killing each other over a tin of pickled fish and the victors dying of botulism poisoning Nathaniel could no longer control himself and he burst out laughing.

'It's not funny,' said Tad. 'It's bleeding tragic, is what it is.'

Nathaniel shook his head. 'It's funny is what it is. Jesus. Clowns killing each other over a tin of fish, bearded fat broads called Dorcas. Man, you couldn't make that crap up.' He guffawed again.

Tad cracked a grin and the he too started to laugh. The two men laughed until they collapsed. They laughed until they were hoarse. They laughed far beyond the humor of the situation because they knew, the real reason that they were laughing was that they were surrounded by dead bodies. Corpses of men that they had just killed.

And they were still alive. So they laughed at the essential insanity of the whole thing. They laughed at life. They laughed in the face of death.

And finally, sated by the blackness of their humor, they walked to their horses, mounted and trotted back to Harry's Farm, leading the spare horses behind them.

They rode in silence and, because Nathaniel took a direct route back, it did not take long. When they arrived back at the farm there was still at least three hours of darkness left.

'Right,' said the marine to Tad. 'Let's get into character. Panic. We were wiped out. We've been shot...'

'We have been shot,' said Tad.

'Well...yes,' admitted Nathaniel. 'True. That's good. More real. Okay, game faces on, lets go. Remember, divide and conquer, we split them up like we did before and take them down.'

The two of them kicked their horses into a gallop and came crashing up to the front gates. Two armed guards stepped out.

'Quick,' shouted Nathaniel. 'Open up. Let us in, then close the gates. They're coming. Move it.'

The two guards hurriedly yanked the gates open and let in the two newcomers and the spare horses.

'You,' Nathaniel pointed at one of the guards. 'Run. Call G-Man. Call out the men. We're going to be under attack very soon.'

The guard ran towards the main farmhouse, shouting as he did. Before he had even got there the front door had been flung open and a bleary eyed G-Man ran out, followed closely by Ratman carrying his sledgehammer. At the same time the other outlaws emerged from their tents and began running towards the boss.

'Soldier boy,' shouted G-Man. 'What's going on?'

'We were attacked,' said Nathaniel. 'It's like they were waiting for us. We both got shot but we made it. Everybody scattered, not sure who made it out alive and who didn't. But I do know that they're following us. Quick, we need to set up a perimeter. Maybe three men at each corner. I'll take a group, Tad can take a group, you take one and Ratman the other.'

G-Man shook his head. 'No way. I want my boys around me. We stay right here, in front of the farmhouse and wait. Strength in numbers.'

'Maybe Tad and I take a few of the boys and patrol the fence,' suggested Nathaniel.

'Hey, soldier,' answered G-Man. 'What the hell don't you understand about this? We stay here and wait. Anyone tries to kill me you boys kill them. Got it?'

There was a chorus of agreement.

Nathaniel stared at Tad.

Tad shrugged.

'Oh, screw this,' said the marine.

He climbed down from his horse, pulled his axe from his belt and stalked towards the group of men standing around G-Man. As he walked forward the air around him wavered with the exothermic heat waves that poured off him. And his body seemed to sparkle as hundreds of tiny bolts of blue-white electricity flashed and rippled over him.

The axe spun. Smashing and cutting through flesh and bone. Some of the defenders opened fire on the marine but, although some of the shotgun pellets did hit him, they did more damage to each other.

Tad stood up in his stirrups, whipped out two throwing knives and launched them at the men that were firing. They both went down, their life's blood gurgling from the slashes in their throats.

Nathaniel continued to cut left and right with great swing arcs of destruction maiming and dismembering with consummate ease.

And then there was only G-Man and Ratman left.

The look of surprise on G-Man's face was almost comical. Ratman, however, seemed almost pleased.

'Told you so,' boss,' he said. 'Can't never trust no Yankee. Didn't I say so?'

He hefted Daisy over his one shoulder and steeped forward.

'Come on soldier,' he said. 'Let's dance.'

He twirled the huge hammer around his head with a speed that amazed Nathaniel. The blobs of bone and gristle that stuck to the steel showed clearly in the torchlight. The muscles in Ratman's overdeveloped shoulders and arms stood out like steel tendons, pushing up taut against his skin. The swinging hammer made a fluting sound as it cut through the air.

Nathaniel shook his head. 'Marine, you dick. Not soldier. Marine.'

Then he simply kicked Ratman in the knee and, as the hammer wielder fell forward, the marine decapitated him with a one arm downward swing of his battle-axe.

'Wow,' said Tad. 'Now that was humiliating. All show and no go. You know, I'm actually a little embarrassed on his behalf. I mean, let's dance, puh-lease. Melodramatic non-starter.'

'Well you weren't much help,' said Nathaniel.

'Was so,' argued Tad. 'I killed the two guys who were shooting at you.'

'Granted,' admitted the marine. 'But only after they'd shot me.'

'Would you have preferred I did nothing?'

'No, said Nathaniel. 'Just, I dunno, maybe you could have chucked a few more knives or something.'

There was the sound of a hammer on a 38 revolver being cocked.

'Stop talking,' shouted G-Man. He waved the revolver at Tad. 'Get off the horse.'

The little man complied, dismounting and walking over to Nathaniel.

'This is your fault,' he said to the marine.

'Oh yeah? How?'

'You should have been watching him.'

'And you?'

'I was busy explaining my battle tactics to you.'

'Shut up!' Screamed G-Man. 'It's time for you both to die.' He raised the revolver and took aim at Nathaniel.

Tad grabbed a throwing knife from his waistcoat and flicked it overarm at G-Man.

At the same time, Nathaniel whipped his axe at the outlaw, using an underarm fling to send it on its way.

The knife struck G-Man in his left eye. The axe hit him in his stomach. Either wound would have killed him outright, so he was dead before he hit the ground.

'Battle tactics?' Questioned Nathaniel. 'Where do you get off chucking a couple of knives at someone and calling that battle tactics? Bloody cutlery tactics, that's all.'

Tad laughed. 'I wonder if they have any of that coffee left.'

'I thought that you didn't like coffee,' said Nathaniel. 'You said that it made you go mental.'

'True,' admitted Tad. 'But, in the current circumstances, who would possibly notice?'

The two of them went into the house, found the coffee pot, threw in a handful of ground coffee and put it onto the wood-stove to brew.

Chapter 25

Commander Ammon looked at the map of the so-called United Kingdom on his desk. Around him stood his three generals and his chief Mage, Seth Hil-Nu. It had been seven months since the Fair-Folk had started their advance across the island and now, when one looked at the map, most of the south-west of it was shaded in Fair-Folk blue. A dark blue line was drawn from Avonmouth in the west, through Bristol and on to Bath, Salisbury and terminating in Southampton on the east coast.

And, as they advanced, the birthing vats in Cornwall continued to produce Orcs at a prodigious rate. The goblins also had upped their breed rate to a phenomenal level as commander Ammon demanded more and more troops in order to fully occupy and control their new world.

The commander now had over three million troops under his command. After consulting with some human advisors, Ammon had decided that the next big step that the Fair-Folk would take was to spearhead through the south of England and occupy London in force. He had seen a number of human cities by now and, according to his sources, London simply dwarfed all of them. It had a large river, many open spaces for cultivation and a proper stone castle. That is where the Fair-Folk would set up permanent residence.

Ammon had planned no fancy tactics. The Fair-Folk would simply mass at Bristol and then march down a road designated M4 right into London. And let woe betide any creature that tried to stop them. One million battle orcs, four hundred thousand goblin archers, thirty trolls, over one hundred thousand constructs and nearly ten thousand humans.

In the last seven months, Ammon's, and thus the Fair-Folk's, attitude towards the humans had changed.

Initially the Fair-Folk had looked to subtly subjugate the humans by the use of glamour and reward. They would offer security, food and in return would use them as servants, thereby voiding the need to create more constructs. It seemed a logical and obvious trade.

However, there was something essentially wrong with the human psyche. Some of them welcomed the Fair-Folk and their offerings with open arms. In fact Ammon was sure that they would have been just as happy even without the use of glamoring. Then there was a second strata of human society that would simply not work as servants no matter how dire a situation they found themselves in. They would literally rather starve to death or at least die trying to fend for themselves.

Then there was the third and, quite frankly, the most disturbing group, albeit it the smallest by far. And this was the group of human dissenters. Not only would they not work for the Fair-Folk, they would simply refuse to accept them at any level.

Ammon felt that the humans had no right to any grievances. He granted that the new Fair-Folk habit of "terrormelding", where the master would induce terror into the human subject and then vicariously revel in their emotions, may have bordered on the un-ethical. But, as far as he knew, the humans were unaware of it. Some had developed suspicions but there was no actual proof.

The same group of humans did not want garrisons posted outside every village and town and they refused to let the Fair-Folk decide on food and crop rationing.

In fact there was now an underground band of human resistance that called themselves 'Humans for Humanity" or "Double H" and their motto was "There will be blood for blood."

Ammon had decreed that anyone found to have even the slightest connection to Double H was to be publicly hung by the neck until dead. As he had explained to his human advisors, it was for the good of all.

Ammon rolled up the map and tied it with a ribbon.

'That is all, good fellows. Prepare the troops, we shall march tomorrow.'

All inclined their heads in respect and made to leave the tent.

'General Atemu,' called Ammon. 'Stay for a while, please. We need to talk.'

The general stood while the others walked out.

'Yes, Atemu. We appear to have a problem. The problem is wide spread, I have merely called you out because the most recent infraction has occurred amongst your Orcs.'

'A problem, my lord? Pray tell.'

'Discipline, general. For the first time in Fair-Folk history we seem to be having a growing discipline problem amongst the battle Orcs.'

Atemu nodded. There was no use denying a fact. 'Perhaps it's a defective batch,' he said. 'Mayhap they breed different here on this earth place.'

'No,' disagreed Ammon. 'This actually started a while back but we of the council have been keeping a lid on it. Some seven months ago, sergeant Gog refused a direct order. When asked why, he said that it was because he had made friends with a human child.'

Atemu snorted with amusement. 'Impossible. Orcs do not make friends. It is beyond their remit.'

'I do not lie,' responded Ammon coldly.

'No. Of course not, my lord,' blustered the general. 'It's just that, well...' he was at a loss for words.

'It has never happened before,' finished Ammon for him.

The general nodded.

'But there has been more,' continued the commander. 'Cases of Orc guards bringing water to human prisoners in their cells. Orcs covering for human servant's mistakes. I have even come across two Orcs playing with human children. Pretending to fight them. Pretending to lose and die. It is most disturbing.'

'It is the human emotions,' said Atemu. Somehow they seem to confuse the Orc's rudimentary control systems.'

'It is not only the Orcs,' said Ammon.

'What? The goblins as well?'

Ammon shook his head. 'No. The goblins seem immune. I am talking about us, dear general. This new habit of terrormelding. In theory I see nothing directly wrong with it. Some humans have been seen to die from the experience, more lately than ever, but that is of no moment. The problem is that many of our elite have become hopelessly addicted to the practice. It needs to stop.'

'How, my lord commander? We can't punish the thin skins. I mean, they don't actually want to do it in the first place. We can't punish ourselves because, well, no Fair-Folk has ever been guilty of transgression of any of our taboos and strictures, as far as I know, so we do not have the necessary structures in place. Anyway, the mere thought of placing a limitation on our own is abhorrent.'

Ammon nodded. 'You speak the truth, general. I am at a loss. For now, let us say that we shall keep a close eye on things. As far as the Orc disobedience goes. We shall stamp down hard on it. All disobedience, however slight, will be met with the hangman's noose. If an Orc is caught fraternizing with a human on any level then the human shall likewise be hung. See to it. That is all. Leave me, collect the troops together. Tomorrow we ride for London.'

General Atemu bowed to the commander.

'It shall be as you have decreed, commander. May the light be with you.'

'And also with you,' returned Ammon.

Chapter 26

Nathaniel watched the sun rise over the farm.

It had been a year and there were over one thousand people living at Harry's farm now. Wooden cabins had been built from scratch, a water tower had been erected and irrigation trenches ran through the fields as did covered sewage drains and piped water to common areas amongst the cabins.

When Nathaniel looked back on the last year it seemed a little crazy. They had created a large village from nothing. It might have been easier and made more sense if they had all simply decamped to an existing village but that wasn't how it had happened.

Harry's Farm had evolved. It had grown organically, albeit with some form of planning. And now it was a thriving, self-contained Mecca.

After Nathaniel and Tad had ridded the farm of the undesirables they had freed Harry and then, at his request, stayed on. The three of them had then planned out how the farm was going to progress and stay safe.

Now, a year later, the inner circle was surrounded by a wooden stockade with stout gates. An outer safe area stood outside the stockade and this was enclosed in coils of razor wire rolled between wooded posts. Further outside the second perimeter was a third one consisting of an eight-foot chain link fence. Inside this final perimeter lay the fields for food cultivation. This third fence was patrolled both day and night by a series of patrols on both horse and foot.

Hunting and foraging parties left the farm on a daily basis and, sometimes, they stayed away for a few days. People were still welcomed with open arms and it had been decided that all comers would be treated with respect as opposed to suspicion. But this time, the respect would be tempered with the steel of weapons. Tough love.

And it was working. For the first time since the pulse, Nathaniel saw mankind's better side on a daily basis and it was an uplifting thing.

'Penny for your thoughts.'

The marine was pulled from his reverie by Tad's greeting.

'Hi, Tad. Nothing much. Just thinking in general. Yourself?'

'Truth be known, my friend,' answered Tad. 'I'm bored out of my mind.'

'What about Janeka? Trouble in paradise?'

Tad laughed. 'Steady on, chap. We're just two adults having a good time. Well,' Tad continued. 'We used to be two adults having a good time. Now we're more, two adults bickering at each other the whole time. Got nothing in common, you see. Nice girl, though.'

'Got any cigarettes?' Asked the marine.

Tad nodded. 'Home made. From Harry's tobacco plants. They're not bad. Here.' The small man pulled out a pouch, opened the neck and extracted a couple of hand rolled finger sized cigars. He put one in his mouth and proffered the other to Nathaniel.

The marine clicked his fingers together and a small flame burned in the air above his thumb. He leaned over and lit Tad's cigarillo, then his own.

'You're getting pretty nifty with that whole conjuring of fire thing,' commented Tad.

Nathaniel shrugged. 'Parlor games. Good for lighting fires and cigarettes, seeing at night. No real power, though. No matter how hard I try. Some sort of mental block. Who knows?'

The two of them smoked in silence for a while.

Then Nathaniel said.

'I'm leaving. Heading north. Milly is safe here. Gramma and the girls have a place of their own. I need to keep going.'

Tad blew a smoke ring. 'Okay,' he said. 'I'll come with.'

'You sure?'

'Sure enough,' said Tad. 'I know that I'm not the framing type. Also, I think that Janeka and I should part ways before things get ugly.'

Right then,' said the marine. 'I'll tell Harry, speak to Gramma and then have a talk with Milly. Not sure how she'll take it.'

'I'll tell Janeka and then prep for the journey, food, horses, weapons. Cigarillos.'

'Don't forget furs,' said Nathaniel. 'I know that it's mild at the moment but as winter comes around again and we head north we're going to freeze our cojones off.'

The two men went their separate ways to carry out their plans.

***

They left late afternoon. Harry had wanted to throw a going away feast but the two friends simply wanted to slip away. There were tears from Milly. She told Nathaniel that she loved him. He told her that he would see her again. She made him promise. He did.

Janeka threw a tantrum and Gramma simply nodded and gave her blessing.

Nathaniel felt bad leaving Milly but he knew that he had to go on. He did not question it as he was being drawn by something far stronger than mere compulsion. His needs were being dictated by his destiny.

And Nathaniel knew that it would be a mistake to look too far ahead, for only one link of the chain of destiny can be handled at a time.

They rode north with a purpose, not rushing, never even rising to a trot, but walking fast. Going forwards. Being on the move once more felt good.

Neither of them talked, easy in the company of their silence. Friends who had hunted and killed and more. Warriors, survivors. Protectors.

The land was devoid of humanity and small game was plentiful. Birds, squirrels, rabbits and deer were thick on the ground. In the last year forests had started to expand. Shooting up unchallenged saplings for acres around every mature wooded area.

They halted an hour or so before dark and put up camp. As was the marine's habit they chose a spot secluded from line of sight, in amongst the trees, well sheltered and close to water. Then Nathaniel set snares for game while Tad collected firewood and built a fire. They had brought victuals from the farm so there was no need to forage.

The rose early the next morning, up with the sun. As it did every morning the aurora borealis shimmered across the skies, creating a light show that had lost its beauty in its familiarity.

Every trap was full of a fat rabbit. Six in all. Nathaniel gutted and dressed them before they moved on, once again traveling due north horses at a fast walk.

Two days later they met two men named Bob. Both were in their late fifties and could have been brothers. Average height, gray bearded, wiry and taciturn. They were camped outside the remains of a tiny village called Whategill. A collection of ten or so houses that had burned down around six months before, judging from the state of plant growth that had taken over.

Both men welcomed Nathaniel and Tad to their fire but Nathaniel noticed they both kept their wood axes close to hand. The marine and the little man offered up a batch of five rabbits to add to the dinner and the four of them sat and chatted over the evening repast.

Both Bobs had worked for a curtain accessory company, curtain rails, hooks, tie-backs, and were on a sales conference being held at a Holiday Inn on the outskirts of London when the pulse struck.

Bob Walter was the regional sales manager and Bob Resnick was the marketing manager. They hailed from Devon, just out side of Cornwall and, as soon as they realized the severity of the pulse they both headed home. Back to Devon and their families. It took them a little under five days to walk the two hundred or so miles to the hometown that they shared. When they got there they could find no sign of their families. Bob Walter's wife and daughter and Bob Resnick's wife and two young sons.

They had searched for months, trudging from place to place, showing photos to all that they met. Hoping. Praying. They never found them. It was as if they had been kidnapped by aliens.

'So,' said Bob Walter. 'We decided to head north. That was some few months back, and here we are. Still heading north.'

'Why?' Asked Nathaniel. 'Why didn't you simply stay where you were. Keep searching?'

Bob raised an eyebrow. 'Because of the Orcs,' he said. 'Don't know about you, but we couldn't stand them. Horrible. Ugly pig-faced bastards. Didn't trust them.'

Nathaniel laughed. 'Yeah, ' he agreed. 'Should never trust an Orc, that's what I've always said.'

Tad smiled as well, appreciating Bob's sense of humor.

'Seriously though, Bob,' continued the marine. 'Why the urge to leave and head north.'

Both Bobs stared at Nathaniel like he was a little simple. Or perhaps simply deaf.

'The Orcs,' repeated Bob Walter. 'And the goblins. And their creepy masters, the so called Fair-Folk.'

There was a long pause as both Nathaniel and Tad started at the Bobs. Eventually Tad spoke.

'Sorry guys, but are we talking Lord of the Rings type Orcs here?'

Both Bobs nodded.

'And goblins. Little squat ugly dudes with green skin?'

Again a duo of nodding agreement.

'Greenish,' said Bob Resnick

There was another pause that was eventually broken by Nathaniel.

'Bullshine.'

I take it that you haven't had the pleasure of coming across them yet?' Asked Bob Walter.

Nathaniel shook his head. 'Sorry, guys, but I simply do not believe you.'

Bob Walter gave a wry grin. Trust me, my friend. If I was going to make crap up I would not have gone for Orcs and goblins and trolls.'

'Trolls as well,' said Tad.

'Yep,' continued Bob Walter. 'Trolls as well. Huge hairy mothers. Anyway, there's millions of the buggers. They've taken control of Cornwall and Devon and the last that we heard they were marching on what remains of London.

Nathaniel burst out laughing. Both Bobs looked a little offended.

'What,' said Bob Walter. 'You don't believe us?'

Nathaniel stopped laughing and shook his head. 'It's not that, fellows. I do believe you, that's what's so bloody funny. You just told me a story about Orcs and goblins and trolls marching on London and I believed you. Man,' continued the marine. 'I really do not know what is going on here but this is some seriously messed up stuff.'

'How come this is the first that we've heard of it?' Asked Tad. 'I mean, where the hell did they come from?'

Bob Resnick shrugged. 'Don't know. Why would you have, I suppose. One thing that we noticed during our trek from Devon to here, there aren't a lot of people left. Disease, starvation, violence, fires. They all took their toll. I'd say, at the maximum, the survival rate after the first full year of the new world was, maybe ten percent. Maybe a little more.'

Tad went pale. 'Jesus,' he whispered. 'Are you saying that, in the last year, over sixty million people have perished?'

Bob Walter nodded. 'Maybe less. Maybe I'm out by a few million.'

'Still,' said Tad. 'Fifty or sixty or more, it makes no difference. It's…it's…'

The little man put his head in his hands. Nathaniel noticed that he was weeping. Slow, fat tears ran down Tad's cheeks. No one spoke for a while.

Nathaniel turned his mind away from the reality. It was too much to absorb. He had, obviously, expected that wholesale death had occurred but he had deliberately shied away from thinking of the actual numbers. And, now that they were out there, he simply refused to think about them. Over time the reality would soak in and he would be able to handle it but he needed to ignore the facts for a while. Because if he didn't then his guilt would overcome him. Being, not only one of the few survivors but also to have been gifted with a hyper-extended life by something that had resulted in the deaths of billions of people worldwide was a complete mind-blast. He had to stay frosty. Prepared. He hoped that he had been saved for a reason and, as such, he could not, he would not, let the awfulness of reality sink him.

The next morning the two couples went their separate ways. Both continued heading north but, without talk or discussion, they simple walked off at different tangents. Because, in a world gone to crap in a handbag, trust ran only skin deep and there was not enough left to go around any more.

They rode for another three days and the weather got colder as they went further north. Small patches of snow lay strewn across the turf. Nature's sno-cones.

And on the forth day they breasted a small hill and came face to face with Hadrian's Wall and the remains of the fort of Cunwarden.

The marine grinned.

'What?'

Asked Tad.

'Been here before said Nathaniel as they rode up to the wall. He dismounted and started to climb to the top of the wall that stood about ten feet high.

'Oh, a long time ago,' said the marine. 'Not exactly sure when but, at a guess, I'd say, oh, one thousand eight hundred years ago. Give or take a hundred.'

The marine stood up on the top of the wall and Tad climbed up next to him.

'See there,' said Nathaniel as he pointed at a hill opposite. 'We charged the Romans from up there. Swept down on them and met there,' he pointed again. 'Used cavalry to break their formations and then slaughtered them to the man. Had a feast afterward. Met a girl.'

Tad stared, open eyed at the marine. 'Just how old are you?' He asked.

'I'm only twenty eight years old,' replied Nathaniel. 'But, at the same time, I think that I have been around, like, forever. You see,' said the marine.

'I am The Forever Man.'

And his voice echoed back from the hills and valleys, reverberating and multiplying, until it sounded as if the very land itself was shouting his name.

The Forever Man had come home.

****

Hi there – I hope that you enjoyed this episode of The Forever Man. If you did, please could you give a review on Amazon…if you didn't then please feel free to email me at my personal email zuffs@sky.com and tell me off!

The next in the series is…

The Forever Man
Book 3: Clan War

Acknowledgements

Polly - thanks for all the hours of editing & valuable input.

Axel - for the readings and the advice.

Mom & Dad & Shirl - for helping me to remember.

Michael Marshal Smith - My mentor and friend, for telling me to keep writing.

Made in the USA
Coppell, TX
06 April 2024